# The Locksmith
## Memoirs of the Lock Man

## R. Iglesias

Story Aperture

# About the author

Born in the Bronx in New York state, at the age of three I left to go live in Florida. Land of eternal sunshine, warmth, alligators and poisonous snakes. Oldest of nine siblings, and space being a premium, I left home at a very early age, fourteen. I started working with locks and keys at this time, and was soon making a living as a locksmith apprentice. Of course I have had other exciting occupations, and I have written about this inside the book.

Now living in Charleston, South Carolina I still work in the lock field in the financial vertical, Banks and financial institutions. I still enjoy the work and hope to do it till I drop. Please enjoy this book and email me a line.

Sincerely, Ray Iglesias

# Contents


Copyrights                           VII

1.  Westshore                         1

2.  Dreams                            7

3.  Abandoned Car                    11

4.  Locksmith 5.0                    17

5.  Amarillo Texas                   23

6.  The Red Haired Giant             29

7.  OOPS!                            33

8.  Opening Day                      37

9.  US Navy                          43

10.  Italians in Italy               49

11.  North Africa                    53

12.  Locksmith 2.0                   57

13.  Big Blue                        63

14.  Jamaican Locksmith              67

15.  Family                          76

| | | |
|---|---|---|
| 16. | Baseball | 83 |
| 17. | Not a Locksmith Story | 87 |
| 18. | Boats, the first call | 95 |
| 19. | Boats and the Wealthy | 101 |
| 20. | Boats, Boats and more Boats | 105 |
| 21. | White Space | 109 |
| 22. | Bits and Pieces | 115 |
| 23. | The Law | 119 |
| 24. | Two Guys | 125 |
| 25. | Business is Business | 129 |
| 26. | Coyotes | 133 |
| 27. | Dimes to Diamonds | 137 |
| 28. | INFORMATION PAGE | 144 |

The Locksmith ICG-85B-00

USCO case # 1-15030250701

ISBN Print 979-8-218 94143-7

E-pub      979-8-218 94144-4

# Chapter 1

# Westshore

WESTSHORE

Being the oldest of nine, with six younger brothers and two smaller sisters, I was always at sorts on how to keep not only myself but those that tagged along with me alive. My parents allowed us immense freedom as children, roaming wherever our feet took us, with no accountability. Growing up in the state of Florida during the fifties and sixties I assumed most families lived by the same rules as my family, being out of the house at first light and not returning home till it was dark. Pack a bologna sandwich,  and all the hours from dark to dark was ours. Growing up on the edge of Tampa there was much to explore, and this lifestyle was conducive for this, especially in the summer.

There is one summer where I have fond memories of an old, flat-bottom, wooden skiff, we discovered one morning washed up in the tall grass that outlined Tampa Bay. With a quick inspection of the hull we deemed her seaworthy, and my three brothers and two friends pushed the boat from the mud. We jumped in, and with long poles to push through the shallow water, we headed out to sea.

The air heavy with heat and mosquitos, no breeze, only encouraged us to push deeper into the bay. I would pole, the skiff, blue and grey in color, around the saltwater shallows of Tampa Bay. The boat did leak and with three of my brothers bailing, like mad, moving water with cups, cans, and bucket, we managed to stay just ahead of the flow of water that seeped through cracks and small holes. Had to keep the old lady afloat.

The hot sun would beat down on our brown bodies, boys wearing only cutoffs and no shoes. Stingrays would chase us through the water and the occasional horseshoe crab would entertain us for hours, crawling aimlessly in the flat bottom of the boat. At times summer storms would grow out in the distant bay and then rush for land, chasing us as we poled and bailed like dervish hedgehogs, pelting us with oversized raindrops that stung and chilled our skin.

We would take refuge in our base camp, located in a wooded area off Westshore Boulevard. A hut built from scrape lumber salvaged, like our boat from the sea. Here we waited out the rain telling endless tales of our imagination with the boom of thunder  and lighting bolts for a backdrop.. This was Westshore and soon the dredging and clearing of trees was going to take place. A large secluded place on the peninsular of Tampa, that later would become million-dollar homes with channels and docks for the rich. But for now, it was ours, all ours.

There was a large oyster shell mound built by Indians, hidden in mystic, with trees draped in Spanish moss close to the water. It had taken many generations of Indians shucking and eating oysters, tossing empty shells in a central spot, through the history of time to build this mound to its substantial size.

The dredgers and developers had started here at the oyster mound, cutting their boat inlets into the land, spewing water, sand, and soil everywhere from large, rusted pipes. In the backwash we would explore and occasionally find an arrowhead. We all had small collections from days spent searching the earth, the thrill of finding and giving each arrow a special name.

One warm summer night came when we decided to camp out. My brothers and a few neighborhood kids, we carefully had planned this for a few days. There was food to consider and blankets. Flashlights and lanterns were stored at the camp site. Only thing left was to lie to our parents about where we would be staying, using each other as alibis.

The day arrived and as a group we headed for Westshore and adventure. I was thirteen, brother Rodney twelve, Randy ten, and Russell was nine, two friends, Jim and Tom were twelve. We all headed out for fun, food and fire.

The fun in adventure comes with the excitement that leads to it. We had made a series of lean-tos from long branches and palm fronds in a half circle and had a very functional stone pit with wood for the fire at our base camp. We had enough wood to survive a winter. We had two tins of Jiffy pop, that popcorn made to cook overheat or open flames, then you rip open the foil and eat. Candy, chips, cookies, and some room-temperature, two litter soda, Mountain Dew Yes, we were going to eat good on this night.

Our camp was fun, and we told stories as we sat around a roaring fire in the ninety-degree heat of summer. We had finished off all our goodies. Empty wrappers and Jiffy pop foil, littered the ground. The darkness of night was upon us. We needed adventure.

The dredgers had finished a long inlet into the earth, about as wide as a football field and twice as long, so we all decided to swim across the saltwater channel in the dark of night. I took the lead with a lit candle in a bottle in one hand, held high to help guide the way, swimming side-stroke with my other hand. I think we were all scared thinking of sharks and assorted sea creatures. Phytoplankton covered our bodies and we all took on this blue green alien glow. We had become sea creatures ourselves. On the other shore we all climbed out, and all agreed that it was fun. No one used the word 'scary,' so we jumped back into the dark abyss and swam back to the other shore and camp.

The stars were bright against the black of sky and the flames of our fire leaped high into the night encouraged by the diesel fuel we had pilfered from a construction site and fed the fire. Diesel fuel that we had found earlier that day at some shack about a mile away.

It was getting late and we were sleepy. We never heard the footsteps of the man as he stepped from the dark into the firelight. A BIG heavy man, in his late twenties, beady eyes darting back and forth trying to take everything in. He was wearing flannel, and it was summer. I knew this was trouble. "Run!" I shouted, and like cockroaches in a restaurant kitchen when you flip on the light, we scattered everywhere.

Most of us evaporated in the dark to hide behind trees. My brother Randy was not so lucky and the big man snatched him by his foot lifting him up in the air. Randy was screaming and the big man told him, "Shut up or I'm going to break some bones."

The Big Man stomped off with Randy tucked under his arm. Slowly we materialized out of the darkness and we gathered in the light of the fire. Shaking with fright, we knew we had to get Randy back, but how? So, we fellowed the big man through the woods quietly, at a very safe distance like butterflies flirting from one tree to another.

Maybe a mile or so he walked and we followed, listening to the grumblings of the Big Man and the wimping of a terrified Randy. Suddenly we ended up at the wooded shack where earlier that day we had liberated some diesel fuel. Crawling through the underbrush, flat on our bellies, we hid under some thorny bushes and watched as he unlocked the padlock on the door of the shack and dragged Randy inside. "What the Hell are we going to do?" my brother Rodney whimpered beside me.

After a few minutes I turned and told them I had an idea. "See those empty glass bottles over there?" both nodded. I told Tom and Rodney, "Fill them up with Diesel fuel from that big tank, like we did this afternoon. Then walk all the way around the shack and wet the walls. I will take care of the rest."

A few minutes passed and then they came back, empty bottles in hand, to babysit Russell. "Okay, now it's my turn." I jumped up and ran to the porch. As I stood by the door I yelled in my deepest child voice, "Mister you smell anything different?"" What" he grunted. "Mister! I soaked your shack in diesel fuel and if you do not send my brother out right now, I am going to light this match and burn it down! With you inside."

After several long seconds, Randy emerged, unharmed, the Big Man stayed inside.

"Now Mister," I again yelled in my deepest child voice, "if you bother us anymore tonight, we are going to come back and finish the job!" Grabbing Randy by the hand, we made a mad dash off the porch. The others scurried out from under the bushes to join us.

We ran the whole distance back to Base Camp. The fire had died out but that was ok. Because now we did something that many would think was not too smart. But we were kids and we sure as hell could not go home in the middle of the night. We grabbed our blankets curled up in our lean-tos and went to sleep. The next morning, we woke up, gathered our stuff, and went home.

We never told our parents, and we never talked about it among ourselves.

The Big Man had never reappeared that night and it was just one more adventure for us from The Westshore.

# Chapter 2

# Dreams

D reams

    I like to tease and say I was born a locksmith; and my first opening was escaping from my mother's womb. I sent her an invoice later in life, she just laughed and threw it in the trash. Actually, I wanted to be an escape artist when I was younger. Reading the life story of Harry Houdini in grade school I became obsessed with ropes, locks, and handcuffs. Houdini's stories amazed me, and I wanted to relive them all.

I trained myself to hold my breath for over three minutes in anticipation of doing some of his water escape tricks. As a child I would have the neighborhood children take rope and wrap it around me and a sturdy tree tying big knots; I would then attempt to free myself. The word attempt is important Often I would fail and struggle with knots long after the  other children went home and the sun dipped below the horizon. My mother, noticing my absence from the dinner table, would go out searching for my whereabouts. Finding me tied to a tree struggling, she would loosen the knots and scold me. All the while I would struggle and cry that, "I almost got it! Leave me alone."

As I grew my career choice turned to a secret agent. Ian Fleming with his James Bond novels, and television shows of spies, corrupting my mind. Dad would insist I consider medicine, his chosen field. He would drag me off to the hospitals where he worked and explain the wonderful mechanics of health care. Sometimes late at night he would lock me in the Morgue as a practical joke. One of his buddies would always be lying on a gurney covered with a sheet and would wait till he locked the door, and was gone, then rise from the table. Adults howling with laughter. I cannot explain why grown men would enjoy making a young kid pee his pants.

Loved watching the television shows 'Man from Uncle' and 'Secret Agent Man.' Reading all of Ian Flemings, James Bond Novels. My brother Rodney and I turned an old laundry room closet into a secret lab. We would collect bottles of chemicals for experiments and make all sorts of mechanical and electrical devices. Parts salvaged from neighbors' trash, to fabricate inventions that allowed our imaginations to soar. We once found a large box of light bulbs. Yes, the light bulbs became our hand grenades. For months we terrorized the neighborhood by throwing exploding lightbulbs from trees, behind cars and at each other. Secret Agents, is what we were.

One day I got this idea that we should make a fire, a big fire. I decided we needed a hole to contain this event and started digging in the back yard of our home in Tampa. All the kids in the neighborhood were out there with me and my brothers; shovels were flying and dirt sailing out of this hole. By nightfall the hole was large and six foot deep. We had to use a ladder to get out. It was an exceptionally good hole.

The next day, waking with anticipated excitement, for the event to come, we decided to fill the hole with anything that could burn. With the help of now dozens of neighborhood kids we tossed wooden boards, paper, many dried out Christmas trees, all types of trash. The mound grew up and out of the hole. It was going to be a blaze visible from the heavens.

Needing some type of catalyst to expedite the blaze, I found a couple of gallons of gasoline my father kept in the garage for the lawnmower. Bringing the gas to our "Burn Pit," I liberally soaked our mountain of flammable debris. Of course, I knew the dangers of fire. I was after all I was almost twelve, the oldest of nine. I cautioned everyone to stand back; this was going to be the biggest and best fire ever.

Climbing down the ladder into the pit I searched for my matches, the stench of gasoline heavy in the dry June air. The couple dozen children around the rim started the countdown. Ten, nine, eight, and I lit the match. Wow, what an explosion! The combination of gasoline, oxygen, and fire from one match created such force, the flames would have been visible from Skylab if this were to happen today. Thankfully, the force of the explosion threw me out of the hole and saved my life. All my little brothers and neighbors, standing on the perimeter of the burn pit, lost their eyebrows from the flames and heat. I was wearing shorts and lost all my hair on my legs, arms. Later I would be bed bound in misery with large water blisters from my toes to my thighs. I was put under martial law and given corporal punishment. Water and food delivered to my cell.

At sixteen my father bought me a used car. Such a nice car it was. An Austin Healey convertible, four speed, two bucket seats, white in color, small and fast. I did not have a driver's license having just turned sixteen, and to this day I do not know what possessed my dad to give a kid a sports car, with no driving credentials. He just tossed me the keys.

I learned how to drive. It took most of the summer of 1968. I could shift and down shift, go fast and occasionally brake. On a scorching summer day, my driving had improved to the point that I promised all the girls in the neighborhood a trip to the beach. Seven of them. All showed up at my house the next morning, and we squeezed into the Austin Healey. All elbows and thighs, towels, and sun lotion we proceeded to Clearwater Beach, outside of Tampa. We almost made it, but flying across the causeway is when the "Fuzz" with flashing red lights pulled me over. As he counted all the heads with disbelief in his voice he said, "Boy, this car only has two seats. Whatcha doing?"

"Going to the beach." I replied. "Nah!" he said. "I want everyone to untangle themselves and climb out of that death trap. Now young man I want you to drive these young ladies back home, One at a time!" It took about three hours, and we never saw the beach on that sweltering summer day. What was strange was he never asked to see my license. Must have known my dad.

I wrecked that car one stormy night out on highway 27. The rain was coming down sideways and the windshield wipers did not work. Hit an oily spot on the highway and the car was sliding first left then right. There was a gasoline tanker truck beside me on the highway and that little Austin Healy slid right under it and came out the other side. Hitting the curb, it snapped the axle and wobbled to a stop. It was towed away. I hitchhiked home and I never saw that sweet car again.

At seventeen I found myself living on my own, my own choice. It was not long before I met someone who would change my life. John Dunn, a locksmith in the late sixties, rescued me in Tampa. He would take me in and become my mentor teaching me the fundamentals of locks and keys. My dreams of being an escape artist or being a secret agent were childish dreams up in smoke, but a locksmith, now that was something I could envision, and my career was off and running.

# Chapter 3
# Abandoned Car

Abandoned car

Coming from a large family of nine siblings, it was easy to get lost in confusing times. Coming home from H.B. Plant High School in Tampa, Florida, late one evening, I was surprised to see that my parents and siblings had packed up and moved out of the house we all had been living in. It is unbelievable that my family had moved while I was in school. Usually they would wait till I got home.

Now my parents had a propensity to move quickly and suddenly, and it was the common theme while growing up to always keep a suitcase packed. I did recall a conversation my mom and dad had earlier about looking for a new 'nest'. Tampa was starting to wear on my dad's nerves, and Miami had a wonderful opportunity. Actually, six months earlier my dad had made the same statement about Miami, and that is how we ended up in Tampa.

Still, coming home from school and seeing your family gone was upsetting. I was just sixteen, and though not my first time being on my own, it was unsettling. Looking inside the empty house, I found my clothes had been left behind. Ten dollars stuck in a shirt pocket. Ten dollars to live on might have sounded cruel, but I did have a job and worked at a local hamburger joint, Steak and Shake, making just enough money to get by.

In the front yard of the house my parents had abandoned, leaning against an old tree, was an abandoned car from the 1940's. No tires, sitting on blocks, it was a Packard, grey and rust in color.

With nowhere to live I moved my meager allotment of clothes to the trunk of this car and when darkness descended, I crawled into the backseat of the vehicle and went to sleep. It was not long before I stopped going to high school. Survival, and adventure, wandering the streets of Tampa, took center stage. I was thin at this time, maybe one hundred twenty-five pounds on a five-foot eight frame.

To survive I kept a loaf of bread and a package of bologna, oh, and a bottle of catsup, hidden in my abandoned car. Allotting myself one sandwich each day, I would tease myself saying, "Nothing better than a home cooked meal. Sometimes I would sing the jingle, "my bologna has a first name, its O-s-c-a-r, my bologna has a last name its M-e-y-e-r."

I was working at Steak and Shake part time and I did manage to find myself a girlfriend in the most unusual of ways. I had started to hustle customers to earn extra cash while waiting on cars as a carhop. Delivering messages from shy high school boys to girls in other cars and playing match maker. It paid one or two dollars per note delivered and the money added up, helping to pay for my bologna sandwiches. On one cool night I was ready to deliver a note from two high school kids to a couple of young ladies parked at the far end of the lot. When I approached the car, she looked up at me from the car window with beautiful blue eyes and long blond hair. Her smile was large and infectious. My heart skipped a few beats, and I fell in love.

I crumpled that note in my pocket, [Sorry boys] and I asked for her number, for me. She was shy of nature but agreeable to a date. I later told those boys that the two girls were off the table and hooked them up with a Mustang parked a few cars down. It was funny because I was living my life on a sharp edge and yet I had a girlfriend whose smile had made me happy.

Roaming the streets to the wee hours of the night, I entered an all-night diner and met the cook behind the counter. He was an Air Force Sargent moonlighting as the short order cook. He approached me and asked if I could work with him at Dobbs House, a diner on Dale Marby Boulevard. He worked the graveyard shift from midnight to eight am. Exhausted from the daytime job he wanted some sleep. and I could cover the wee hours between midnight and six. It was a new chance for me to make some money.

"Sure," I responded, and going behind the counter, he taught me how to make breakfast. Flipping eggs, scrambling eggs, toast, waffles, bacon, and sausage. He was a good teacher and after one night he said, "tomorrow you are on your own," and off he went to sleep in the stockroom.

I was a naive kid back then and the Air Force Sargent took full advantage of me. He never paid me for working those nights. I did approached the Dobbs house management during the day, and because I was not on the "Books," they refused to pay. To even the score, later in the week I returned to the Dobbs House Restaurant and found the place empty except for a young waitress/cook. Striking up a conversation, it was not long before I asked her if she would like to make some extra cash.

Please keep in mind that I was young, but my hobby was locks and keys, and I was very adept at this. I had wanted to be Harry Houdini as a kid remember? I made my own lock picks and studied locks, so I was in my field of expertise when I suggested to her that I open the lock box on the Junk Box and we divide the coinage. Of course, she agreed, and we each made off with a little over sixty dollars each, in quarters.

I digress. While working for the Air Force Sargent who slept like a baby in the stock room, one night, it was around four or five am,  a young man entered the diner and sat at the counter. The place was empty and while cooking his breakfast we struck up a conversation. The sun was starting to come up, and he asked if I had a girlfriend. Of course I went into detail about my blue-eyed sweetheart. The conversation turned to what gifts I had bestowed on her, and I realized I was a pauper. No gifts, just some poetry and prose proclaiming my love to her, no gifts.

This is when he said he had a cool idea. He told me he had a polaroid camera in his hotel room across the street. He was willing to bet my girlfriend would love a photo of me as a gift and this would only take a few minutes. 'Wow! What a great idea.' I thought and agreed to meet at the end of my shift.

Reaching the hotel room, he asked me to pose by the bed in the room. Suddenly he smiles and says you should remove your shirt and show her your muscles. What the heck, and I think she might enjoy that. I unbuttoned my shirt and threw it on the bed. He aims the camera to take a photo, the built in flash goes off and the undeveloped photo slides out the front of the camera. He is waving the film in the air to speed up the process of development, then says "you should give her a sexy photo. Unbuckle your belt and unbutton a few buttons on those bell bottoms."

I am very tired from working all night. I agree and hope this blond creature that has my heart will appreciate all this. I strike a pose with no shirt, my belt and fly of my pants open, and just a hint of curly pubic hair showing. I am a sinewy, deep brown piece of shoe leather with blue jeans falling off my legs. She will love me.

Suddenly the young man throws his polaroid camera on the bed and tries to grab me around the waist. He is trying to pull me down,

I realize quickly what he is trying to do, and pushing him to one side I twist around and grab my shirt off the bed. Holding my pants up with one hand, I made a hasty retreat out the door and ran across the parking lot. Stopping for a moment by the dumpster, to finish dressing, I turn and from the doorway I hear the man yelling, "Please come back, you forgot your photo."

# Chapter 4
# Locksmith 5.0

Locksmith 5.0

One of the most misunderstood professions is Locksmith. What they do and how they do it remains a mystery to most adults, and Locksmiths are fundamentally to blame for the cloak of secrecy that engulfs them. Most locksmiths do not share knowledge with others. They believe they are members of a secret guild with guarded trade secrets. Many older locksmiths will not share knowledge with their own staff, hobbling them in performing the duties expected of them. Of course, this is slowly changing as more educated and young people enter the field. Also, associations like 'Associated Locksmiths Of America' through educational classes and seminars are slowly changing the visual perception of those who work in this chosen line. Electronics, cameras, alarms, and computers have joined the arsenal of lock work. Interfacing this with mechanical hardware is blurring the lines of the status quo job description.

Locksmiths do more than unlock automobiles and cut keys, a whole lot more. The trade is broken up into many categories, Automotive, Residential to start. There is also Commercial, Industrial, Marine Hardware, Aviation, and all have subsections like Electronics,

Mechanical, Sales, Service, or Teachers. Levels of competence exist in all these categories and to master just one may take a lifetime.

There is a trend now for locksmiths to call themselves Security Consultants, as if a fancy title is going to change how people perceive their status. Locksmith suits me simply fine. I dare say I have made a decent living and will continue to do so, no matter what you call me.

If you are not unlocking cars or opening homes for absent minded people, what do locksmiths do? Good question. Commercial work can encompass a variety of skills. Installing complex locking devices for asset protection, closed circuit camera systems, safe sales, and service. You might work on the alarm installation, monitoring, or integration of all these systems. One of my favorite tasks was designing large master key systems for large buildings, airports, banking chains, condos and the list goes on.

Designing a key system for clients with grand needs requires a sharp eye for detail. Care must be taken not to cross-key; that is someone's key opens someone else's lock. Master keys need to work where you have designed them to, and key expansion must be incorporated into the design. A lot of math is used for this. Keys are translated into a number sequence, and pages and pages of numbers are generated to issue all keys with specific values and identification codes. Care must be taken. This used to take pages and pages of numbers all by hand. Today the modern locksmith uses a computer to achieve the task, yet I think you should still know how these systems are generated because I have caught computers with glaring errors.

Industrial locksmithing requires other specialized skills. I worked for a Federal Detention camp in the Everglades. Security is layered in these arenas and electronic locks are just part of the system. These locks need to stand up to the abuse of people constantly tampering with them. Shoving trash into them and criminals trying to defeat them. The cameras in the communal areas are installed in metal cages to prevent vandalism and still inmates will do things like throw human feces at them to clog the lens. My least liked job was cleaning those cameras.

Industrial locksmiths maintain locks, doors, door frames, closures, hinges, and anything else management can squeeze into your job title.

Automotive locksmithing is where most of us start our careers, that and residential. Automotive locksmithing now is a field all to itself. It used to be just making a key to start a vehicle. Now they use credentials with passive and active interfaces, laser cut, two and four track keys with embedded chips and program codes to open the onboard computers. Autos are the most advanced evolving field in this business. Residential is a wonderful way to get introduced to our work. Can you make money working on homes and doors? After all you are competing with the Big Box stores, but it is possible to carve out a niche here. Selling and installing designer hardware is one way or pushing High Security Locks for a increased level of security.

Had a client call me one day to recommend some locks for his home. When I arrived, I surveyed his home and counted just over fifty doors. I recommended a high security deadbolt that had a cost of two hundred and fifty dollars a unit. His question was, what color do they come in? Needless to say, he chose an antique nickel finish, and he did all fifty plus doors. The twist to this job came about four weeks after we had finished the installation with a hefty profit. He called me and complained about the finish he had chosen. Please he begged can you get me fifty new locks in just a nickel finish; I will pay your rate? What could I say but, yes! Sold the guy fifty plus more locks at the same price, with installation.

What about the old locks, I asked him. Get rid of them, please. I do not need them, was his answer. I had removed the locks carefully and returned them to the boxes I had just taken the latest product out of. When I returned to my shop I rekeyed the locks with individual high security keys, placed them on the shelf and sold them all over the next year. Yes, I made a profit from that job.

I opened my first locksmith business in 1977. All I had was an old Dodge van and five hundred dollars. I was working for one hundred and thirty-five dollars a week repairing washing machines and refrigerators. The first night the advertisement came out in the phonebook I ran a couple or three calls and made over four hundred dollars. The next day I quit that appliance repair job and never looked back.

Today the work is different, more high-tech, more specialized tools needed to accomplish a call. Related expenses like license fees, insurance, are through the roof. Yet there are ways, because I still see many new young faces entering the field and I find that pretty cool. I will only tell those young people to keep learning, taking classes and courses. Knowledge is real wealth, and no one can steal that from you.

In 1969, I told my mom I was leaving home. She asked with tears in her eyes, "What are you going to do?" "Why I am going to become a locksmith." I answered back. She laughed and laughed with more tears streaming down her face. "You are going to make a living cutting keys?" At that time keys could be bought at three for a dollar. "Yes mom." I replied and I left her house.

In 2005 I threw an extravagant party for my daughter turning fifteen and my mother finally came to see me after all those years. The next morning, she came for breakfast to my home. A large home with sculpted pool and waterfalls, A large boat in the drive and my daughter's birthday present, a new BMW parked in the driveway. As we finished breakfast with the family, she took me by the arm and pulled me to one side. "Ray" she whispers, "How in the world did you get enough money to afford all this?" "Why Mom," I replied, "cutting keys."

# Chapter 5
# Amarillo Texas

A marillo, Texas   July,1970

I was eighteen, having returned to live at my parent's house in Miami, and already I was desperate to be back out on my own to get my feet underneath me as a self-sufficient man.

I had met a young girl wearing bell bottom jeans and a flowered blouse. She was as desperate as me to leave South Florida and escape overbearing parents. She drove an old Ford station wagon with room for lots of stuff. She suggested Amarillo because she had an older sister living there. This was the 'Hippie Days' and not a big thing to hook-up and travel. Also, she had the station wagon, so I agreed to go, why not.

I did traveled from Miami to Amarillo and found myself standing in the hot dry air of an arid town, in the middle of the panhandle of Texas. This was the wild west. As I looked around everyone had large Stetson Cowboy hats sitting on their heads and most carried weapons, either a rifle slung over a shoulder or six shooter strapped to a thigh. Some had both.

Amarillo was a strange place for me, coming out of Florida wearing bell bottoms and flower printed shirts. My hair was long, curly, and wild; I was skinny as a stick and just loved that Rock and Roll music.

The Proverbial Hippie that parents would tell their daughters to stay away from. Amarillo was filled with long guns, cowboy hats, boots of alligator skin, and Cadillacs. This was downtown Amarillo, yes, I thought, I was going to fit right in.

We found a nice little upstairs apartment downtown across from a beautiful park. Except for the blood on the carpet and a chalk outline of a body, it was a cozy warm nest. Now I needed a job. After searching the newspaper want ads, I found an advertisement for a locksmith at a downtown shop called, 'Tom and Roy's Gun and Lock shop.' It was the only lock shop in town, and I was starting to feel lucky, finding my dream job in the heart of the dust bowl. I made a phone call to the owner, Tom. Tom and his wife Bell both agreed to meet with me, and sit through an interview. They came to my apartment shortly after five. When he knocked on my door, I opened and greeted this elderly couple dressed in plaid cowboy shirts with rhinestone buttons, matching cowboy hats and boots.

"Howdy son" said Tom and then introduced himself and his wife. I thought to myself, 'Son? What are you, my daddy.' But I stayed cool and quiet. Of course, he kept calling me 'son' through the entire interview and I kept reminding him my name was Ray. He did offer me the job, and I was thrilled to find work in the field of my desire. As he was leaving, he said there were two conditions I would need to meet. I would need to get a haircut and wear a cowboy hat at work.

"I refuse to wear a cowboy hat!" I yelled, figuring that I had just lost that job. Tom, unfazed, turned back at me with a Texas smile, said, "Ok son, just be sure and get that haircut." He was so smart, I think he had just out maneuvered me.

The next day I had to find some place to get a haircut. Back then they cost two dollars and after checking my coins I had just enough. It was Summertime and walking down the dusty hot streets of Amarillo,

I could see the reflection of my long curly hair in the shop windows. It had been many years since I had seen a barber, or even a comb. 'What was I doing?' I thought. My brain cried out, 'No, No, No!' then the other half of my brain screamed, 'you need a Job, Job, Job!'

After walking for some time, I found one of those red, white, and blue spinning poles in front of a small storefront, a barber shop. In the hot afternoon heat, I took a big gulp of air, pushed the screen door open and stepped inside. My eyes slowly adjusted to the dim interior, and I focused on six incredibly old men sitting in wooded cane back chairs against a fly splatted wall. A paddle fan labored slowly against the heated air moving little white hairs in whirlwind patterns on the hard concrete floor. In the center of the room a single barber's chair of aged cracked black leather contained a large man of some advanced years getting scalped by an old, and I do mean old, thin barber with horn rimmed glasses balanced on the tip of his nose.

Standing there with a pair of scissors in his hands, he stopped and looked at me, up and down. The six old men had stopped talking and moving, maybe even breathing. I was their first experience at seeing a hippie this close. I swear my Bell bottoms were clean and I had even removed the flowers from my hair. The only noise was the squeaking of the paddle fan slowly spinning.

The old barber turned to me and after a long moment of hesitation said, "We don't do your kind in here." Wow, I thought, this was going to be hard. With a weak smile I squeaked, "Sir, I need a haircut, a real short haircut. So I can get a job." The six men in the chairs lined against the wall, the crusty barber and the paying client seated in the barber chair, all just stared at me and time stood still for an eternity.

Finally, his lips twisted into a demonic grin, "Well," he drawled, in a thick Texas accent, "maybe we can just make this work out." Glancing over at the 'old six,' their heads were bobbing up and down in agreement, and the barber added, "I don't want no talking back and you will take it like a man."

"Yes sir," I agreed. "I will just sit here at the end of the line till it's my turn." The old six started talking all at once, insisting that I move to the front of the line. They were in no hurry, they claimed. The man in the worn-out barber chair, jumped up, whipping off the cape, scattering little white hairs to join other little white hairs already on the floor. "Here Son, climb in the chair, please, I'm all done here." And the old six like a church choir chimed in, "climb in the chair son, climb in the chair."

Now I have swum with bull sharks and walked down dark alleys in poorly lit parts of big cities but for the first time I was truly scared. Yet I climbed in that chair and the cape came swooping down around my neck. The barber stood quietly for a few minutes, eyes closed, saying a silent prayer.Then opening his eyes and raising the scissors like an orchestra conductor with a baton, he began his work.

Hair was flying everywhere making it difficult to breathe. The paddle fan groaned loudly to keep the air moving and time slowed down to a crawl. There was the buzz of clippers and the slap of a razor being sharpen on leather. The heat, the hair, was heavy in the air, yet none of the old six left.

Finally, the old barber shouted, with glee and vigor in his voice, "Done! It is done!" from a large mountain of deep brown hair. The old six, which was seven now, jumped to their feet shouting with laughter and giving each other the "high five's.' As I stood, they surrounded me with slaps on my back and jubilant laughter. It was as if under all my hair they had discovered one of their own, and it was me. The barber shoved a large round mirror in my hand and the men were all shouting, "Look, Look!"

I looked into the mirror, and I did not know who that was. I thought about crying, but slowly I realized it was not that bad, I could live with that guy. Slowly I started to smile and from my lips the words, "Not bad." escaped. The old six, now seven and the barber, started jabbering again and giving each other their high fives. It was possible one or more might keel over with the excitement.

I politely asked the barber how much I owned him as I started counting coins out in my hand. The Barber beaming proudly said, "Put your money away, son." They sure loved calling me son in Texas. "Hell, there is no charge. I ain't had that much fun in a bunch of years."

Saying goodbye to all my newfound friends, I stepped out into the heat of Amarillo. Glancing at my reflection in a storefront window I see the new radical me staring back, and I muse aloud, "The haircut is not that bad, maybe I ought to go check out some boots and a cowboy hat."

"Nah! Let us not get crazy!"

# Chapter 6
# The Red Haired Giant

The Red-Haired Giant

In Amarillo Texas, I worked my first real locksmith job in a lock shop named 'Tom &Roy's Gun and Lock.' This was in 1970, and this is where I got a brutal haircut for the right to have gainful employment. {That story in a previous chapter} Now I was a sixties child coming out of Tampa and Miami with long hair and a passion for Peace, Love, and Harmony.

Amarillo scared me a little in 1970 because it was a western town. Cowboy Boots and Stetson Hats were everywhere, and many of the people openly carried Revolvers strapped to their hips, or rifles slung over their shoulder. Tom and Bell, owners of the shop hired me giving me a chance to learn the trade. Hearts of gold those two.

The first day they asked me to make a key for a lock. "Of course," I replied. And placing the lock into a vise I took a Pippen file [a tear shaped, fine cut file} and a key blank. Inserting the key into the lock and wiggling it up and down the small pins inside the lock left marks on the blank. I would file these 'scratches' and insert the key again. After five minutes I had made a working key, holding it up I beamed a big smile and the group watching burst out laughing.

Tom, still chuckling, said, "well I guess that is one way of doing it. Obviously, you know the mechanics of locks and how they work, so we are going to keep you and teach you. Also have you given any more thought to that cowboy hat?"

Within a few months I was making keys for cars and rekeying locks. I was assigned a van equipped with key machine and blanks and sent out on the road to run Service calls. The weirdest thing about this van was the radio only played Country Western music. Now I was a Jimmi Hendrix, Led Zepplin kind of guy, not a Porter Wagner, Dolly Parton type. Amarillo Texas at this time was not a Haven for Hippies.

I have a gift for the trade, and I immersed myself fully into their tutelage and learning. In 1970 I was making one hundred dollars a week. I look back and realize I was paying my dues. in life sometimes you need to sacrifice, stick with something, and suddenly one day you will find yourself at the top making the big money. Next year.

I loved running Service and when a call came in for an early morning home rekey, I jumped at the opportunity. Driving out to the edge of town I found the house hidden behind a white picket fence and a yard full of six-foot-high weeds. From the house Jethro Tull was blasting, 'finally someone with my taste in music.' The door was open, so I poked my head in and yelled 'Locksmith!'

From the darkness of the house a woman's voice raspy with age, and I later learn alcohol use, screamed, "Come In!"

My eyes had to adjust to the darkness of the room and after adjusting, I made out the shape of a large woman. She was not only tall but built heavy, sitting in a rocking chair, she had a record player next to her cracked up to its highest volume level. On her head she had a mountain of bright red-hair in her left hand she gasped a bottle of Jack Daniels, almost empty. From her right hand swung a large Colt 45 revolver.

Pointing the revolver at my chest, to emphasize her question, she asked "Are you a good man? Cause I need me a good man right now!" She had to be in her fifties, and I was only eighteen so you may understand why I was overwhelmed with fear. I replied to her that I was only a locksmith and started backing to the door. "Well, you really look like a good man to me." she exclaimed.

I focused on my job and unscrewed the lock from her door, asking how many keys she would need. "I need a good man she replied." "OK, Ma'am I'll make you four keys." Walking out to my service van I climbed in the back and started disassembling the lock to rekey. I could hear in the background the music change to Led Zepplin's Stairway to heaven. I had a lot of little parts in my hands, yet I realized I should hurry.

The back door was open to my service van, and I never heard her creep up on me. She suddenly jumped in the back door screaming, "Got You!" I threw all the parts up in the air and they flew everywhere. At eighteen I could have had my first heart attack. She was still holding the Jack Daniels bottle and waving the colt forty-five around. "I'm part Injun and part Irish." As she laughed and laughed. "you're a damn Red-Haired giant" I shot back. "Now don't be nasty" she continued. "I can see you are a good man, Mr. Locksmith. finish that darn lock and come back inside, I need a good man." I thought,' you sure talk a lot for an injun.' I did not say that aloud. Finishing the lock, I replaced it on her door under a barrage of sexual innuendos and 'red-haired giant' laughing.

As I was preparing to leave, Federal Marshals pulled up to the curb in a black sedan. Two men jumped out yelling, we got us a warrant for the arrest of, 'one tall red-haired giant', for the use of a firearm inside a US postal office.

I stood in awe as she was placed in handcuffs and led away, minus one bottle of Jack Daniels and one Colt 45. As I stood there talking to the Federal Marshalls, they told me the story of how she had bought a gun the day before and then stood in a Post Office waving her Colt 45 in the air demanding immediate service to buy some stamps.

"Can I ask where she bought this weapon?" I inquired. "Sure" the agent responded, "At a local gun shop, Tom and Roy's Gun and Lock, in downtown Amarillo."

# Chapter 7

# OOPS!

OOPS!

The man kept screaming into the phone that he needed the safe opened today. It was Friday and his staff wanted to get paid. Checks, money, and documents were all locked inside. It was the late Sixty's, and safe work was new to me, I was trying to gather as much information as possible, but all the man could say was that it was an old safe. "Old safes are easy, right?"

"I don't know," was my response. The truth, I was only eighteen and had never opened a safe. Sure, I knew the basics and had read a few books with lots of pictures. But to actually put a sharp drill bit against a safe door, I had not a clue. I tried to explain that my experience was limited, hiding the fact that it was nonexistent, but the man on the phone was desperate and continued to insist that I come over.

Maybe I should have just said no. Instead I said tell me more about this safe. "Ok" he started, "this safe I bought off some Army dudes five or ten years ago. It was used during World War Two in DC and had outlived its usefulness. I had paid a hundred dollars for it, and it had worked well up until this morning. Now the combination will not dial in, and my staff is desperate to get paid. Look, my office is located on the seventh floor and is just down the street from your shop. Please come try, you are my only hope."

"Ok, no promises but I will head your way and see you in half an hour."

Thirty minutes later I walk into his office and was met by a middle-aged balding, red faced man. He grabs my free hand and pumps it up and down. He is happy to see me. The office has two rows of desk that stretch back to a glass enclosed room. Through the open door I see a large black safe about four foot in height sitting on casters. "Is that my client?" I joke with the man. "Yes. Oh, hell yes." is his response.

I walk over spin the dial and yank on the handle, Yhupp, it is locked. I ask him for his combination; he hands over a scrap of paper with numbers written down. I sit down in front of the safe and begin dialing the numbers, without luck. I try variations but not knowing what I am doing it seems to be a futile exercise.

Turning to the man I say, "Only thing I can think of is drilling a hole and punching the back plate and wheel pack off the lock. This should work but remember I have limited experience with these old vaults." "Yes! Yes! We got to go for it," he implores me. Running down to my service van I grab tools, a large hammer and drill motor. Taking the elevator back up to the seventh floor I enter the office and lay my tools out on top of the mini vault.

I pretend to know my exact location for the first hole; I tell myself I am taking an educated guess based on experience. We all know the truth; I'm squeezing my lucky Rabbit foot in my pocket.

I drill the hole and feel the bit penetrate the door and enter the void of the lock body. With less than two inches in the void I feel the bit bumping the back lid of the lock. "Oh my gosh!" This is what I want, I can not believe I am this lucky.

Office personnel by this point have stopped working and most have crept close to the opened office door to see this skinny kid work his magic on the big black bad safe. "What's next?" ask the balding red-faced man. "Watch." I whisper.

Taking an eight-inch threaded steel rod I slid it into the drilled hole. Encountering the back plate, I took my three-pound sledge and began to whack the end of the rod. After several blows I feel the back plate break and hear parts of the wheel pack fall harmless down inside the safe door.

I am so happy and proud to have opened my first safe, I look up at the balding man and all his employees peeking over his shoulders, I give a big smile, turn the safe handle, and pull open the door.

I am Blind! I cannot see from my eyes, snot is pouring out of my nose, my throat is burning and if I can stop coughing for a minute, I will vomit. I begin to claw my way to the open door. I can hear people screaming and crying. Behind me everyone pushing to get out of that office. Office workers stumbling and rolling down the emergency exit stairwell, No one is waiting for the elevator. There is no orderly evacuation just hysteria and panic.

What have I done? Opened Pandora's Box.

Whatever came out of that safe quickly spread through the building. Within Fifteen minutes the building was empty and the Fire Department, wearing Hazmat suites and breathing apparatus, arrived and swarmed the office tower looking for cause and effect.

After much discussion and head scratching the fire department was able to examine the old, World War II safe. The epic- center of the disaster. After setting fans and airing the building they checked the small vault door. Removing the inside door plate finding a glass vial, broken. The vial had broken when I punched the wheel pack off the lock crushing the glass. The vial had contained a healthy dose of mustard gas that had aged over the years increasing its potency, like fine red wine, until its release on the seventh floor office. It filled the interior of the safe with gas. When I swung the door open it rushed out in a big cloud, everyone on the seventh floor was affected, men and women, thankfully no children were present. The gas had leached through the building losing some of its potency, but with enough punch to send everyone out onto the street with coughing fits and wet eyes.

By nightfall everything had returned to normal. Fire department had left and the business man met payroll for its staff. And me, well, I was told, 'you never forget your first'.

# Chapter 8

# Opening Day

Opening Day

Us locksmiths have a funny saying, 'Every day is opening day when you are a locksmith.' This is true. We locksmiths open everything from cars, to safes, to safe deposit boxes. Sometimes I am asked to open a jar of pickles or maybe some spaghetti sauce. It really does not matter what, we just open it. Now opening stuff for people can, at times, lead to peculiar situations and I want to share a few with you.

Cars are by far the most common request that we encounter. Most locksmiths start out opening cars and with training and education advance into more complex job skills. Locksmithing is multi-faceted, broken down into four basic levels, the skill sets are Automotive, Residential, Commercial, and Industrial. Sometimes a person can specialize in just one of the four. Sometimes they can evolve into an even more narrow field. An example like working in the financial vertical, the world of banking, or just bank safe work, large vaults, time clocks, money chest, and night depository safes.

I had, at a time in the nineties, specialized in marine hardware. Had to work in the metric system as all boat hardware is made in

European countries. This required the ability to convert back and forth between metric and standard quickly with no room for errors. Spending long hours working on mega yachts was tedious, owners and captains demanding perfection. I worked on nothing smaller than sixty feet, preferring yachts 120 feet or longer. Yachts were extremely difficult, dealing with rich snobs and miserable captains. Still, I found rich people's toys extremely rewarding to work on, [Had to use a wheelbarrow to get the money to the bank]. I hope to write some mega yacht stories a little later in this book, so keep reading.

Back to strange openings. I got a call one afternoon from a young man that had locked his keys inside his new Buick. He impressed on me that he was an important man and terribly busy, could I hurry. Appreciating his urgency, I raced to his site which was just under thirty minutes away. I did not run any lights, but I did hustle. He was on the phone when I arrived, obviously an important phone call because all he could manage was to point at the car. Looking at the car I turned back to him and gave him the international sign for Money by rubbing my thumb against my fingers. I needed payment before I could begin. With an exasperated sigh he tossed me his credit card, and I processed the payment. I returned his card and he gave me the international hand sign for hurry up. Not wanting to waste anymore of this man's precious time I walked around the Buick to the passenger side of the car. Reaching into the car through the open window I pulled the keys from the ignition, [yes, he had left the passenger window down and had never checked.] walking back around the car I placed the keys in his outstretched hand and silently mouthed the words, Thank you. He dropped his phone as I drove off and waved goodbye. He gave me the one finger salute for, "I hope I never see you again."

When opening cars people will sometimes act irrationally. They can be embarrassed, in a hurry or do not want to pay for your service. I have a philosophy of payment up front unless their wallet or purse is locked in the car. I usually park right behind the vehicle to prevent them from jumping in the automobile and taking off. I once witnessed a little old lady beat a tow truck driver out of his fee. After opening the car, she quickly slid behind the wheel and roared out of the parking lot, leaving her motorized handicap shopping cart stranded in the middle of the road. What is bad is that some people will call four or five locksmiths for help, working with the one that is fastest on arrival. When I see people like this I refuse to participate in that folly. Sometimes we gather and after a discussion, we all agree to drive off. Now the customer is really locked out. Good luck now trying to find some assistance.

I had a client that called once and when I arrived, he had this beautiful Mercedes with the doors locked, the key fob was in his hand. "The battery is dead, and this fob no longer works," he cried. "Can you get in and help me start the car?" I felt kind of sad for the guy as I took his remote and showed him the emergency bypass key hidden inside the fob. By pressing a small button, the key slid out and worked nicely on the driver's door lock. By holding the fob next to the "press to start" switch, he was surprised to see the car start up. I still collected my fee. I could not feel guilty because the guy lacked this knowledge, and after all the man was driving an extremely expensive Mercedes.

The second most common job for young locksmiths is home lockouts. And the service calls run the gambit from someone with only a towel wrapped around them, to jealous boyfriends trying to catch their girlfriend cheating. I was asked to open an apartment for a landlord one time and after pounding on the door for several minutes, I got down on my knees and started to 'pick' the lock with my tools of the trade. Now I am an exceptionally good lock picker, and this door was no match for my skills. As I turned the picked cylinder,

I also turned the knob to retract the latch. I push the door open a crack, maybe two inches. That is when a double-barreled shotgun slid down the door frame and stopped, resting on my nose, pointing at my face. From inside the dark apartment came a  Big Man's deep voice. A voice that slithered out of that two-inch crack. "Boy, just what do you think you're doing?" The words filled with dread and smelling of whiskey, sour urine and danger. This is when you honestly reevaluate your career choice and your brain whispers to your spine, 'I wish I had chosen another profession.'

Working in Amarillo, Texas, July 1971, it was a hot sizzling summer. I got a call from one of our favorite customers, Mrs. Borden. Mrs. Borden, God love her, would lock herself out of her house twice, three times a week. She was such a "regular" at getting locked out that we kept a key hidden to her house under a flowerpot in her garden. Sometimes if we were too busy to respond we would explain on the phone to her that she had left the key, you know where, under the flowerpot and that would expedite her getting back inside her home.

One day she called the shop and told me she was locked out of her house and to please rush over. When I arrived, she was nowhere to be seen, so I walked up to her big porch and rang the bell. A few minutes passed and then she opened her front door. Not surprised I said, "Well that's good, I see that you got into your home." and started to leave. "Wait" she shouted in her little old lady voice, "it's not this house I'm locked out of; it's my house on the other side of town."  Now Mrs. Borden was a very wealthy lady, and it was quite possible she had more than one house. "Yes" and she smiled, "my second house I seldom use, but today I need to go over and do some cleaning inside. Not sure of the exact address, but I will be happy to guide you."

"Ok," and with Texas pride added, "why don't you ride with me. Here, take my hand, I will help you climb into the passenger side of the van." Once she was situated, I ran around and got behind the wheel. "What's the address?" I asked. She replied by pointing down the street and saying, "I'll direct you, young man just go to the corner and make a left." Zooming off, I got to the corner, making a left. Soon I was headed across town and for about Fifteen minutes I listen intently to her directions. I was becoming suspicious because her directions were taking us in circles, Zigzags, and squares. She was starting to become nervous and unsure of where we were going. The light bulb finally went off in my head.

I turned to her and said, "Mrs. Borden, please relax, I just remembered where your second house is." Turning the van around, I headed back to where I had picked her up, after fifteen minutes of windshield time, we were soon back in front of her house. She was so excited she cried out, "Yes that is it! You found it." Helping her down out of the van I said "congratulations you are home. I will see you later." "Wait," she cried, "I am locked out. That is why I called you." Checking the front door, it was locked and laughing I said, "Mrs. Borden, check your pockets for a key." She had no key. Peeking in the front window I could see her keys on the small table by the door, and yes, she was locked out, again. Unbelievable, I thought as I climbed off the porch and into her flower garden, now which flowerpot did we hide that key under?

# Chapter 9

# US Navy

In the US Navy,

Being a sailor and having your first ocean voyage is very cool. The feel of the ship under your feet moving with the roll of the ocean, moving into unknown territory for some formidable adventure, the unexpected, there is nothing like it. Learning a new language, I call Navy talk, bulkhead for wall, bunk for bed, even Bug juice for Kool-Aid. Port to Starboard and terms like forward or aft were essential to finding things like the head {bathroom} or your bunk in the middle of the night. Stairs were referred to as ladders and doors as hatches, and only the vilest rookies would let their feet touch the stair treads between decks. Grabbing the rails and sliding down was the only way to traverse to lower levels.

At first the ship would rock slightly in the flat coastal seas and most greenhorns would vomit at this point and curse their luck. but as the ship headed into deep water and the swells would grow in size. The ship would bite into the sea and find a rhythm in her roll and pitch. The ship becoming an exotic dance between ocean and wind.

The sonar techs would activate the sonar gear and the endless ping of sound traveling out into the ocean in search of some Submarine signature, would echo endlessly. This was the music to the dance as waves crushed against the steel hull and the screw powered by steam turbines set the beat, it was easy to sleep content in your small bunk under warm blankets.

At ten every night they would announce over the PA that the smoking lamp was extinguished and lights out in all berthing . compartments, but if sleep were not in your mind, you could always find a card game going on somewhere in the bowels of the ship. I would always find a game of hearts or spades being played in the sonar room, which backed up to my electronic shop. Where we shared a door. and hours could be spent laughing and dealing cards until midnight. At midnight, the Mess Hall would put out the "Mid-Rats" midnight rations. And Yum! Yum! It was always good stuff with cold glasses of "Bug Juice."

I should mention that every night at eight pm they would show a good movie on the mess deck with plenty of popcorn and of course sweet red Bug Juice. Spaghetti Westerns were always the favorite, but an occasional Romance would squeeze in. There is no TV at sea, so the movies were always popular.

If you wanted to go out on deck at night you could, but you would pass through sets of black-out curtains to contain the ship's interior light, and smoking outside was forbidden. You can see the glow of a cigarette tip over five miles out at sea.

It was always very dark at first, then your eyes would adjust, and the dazzling array of stars would light your world and take your breath away. I guess your pupils would grow to the size of nickels and the heavens would open up. If you made your way to the fantail, the aft outside deck of the ship, you would always find the fantail watch. One lone sailor with a set of headphones strapped to his head, talking to the bridge while looking aft. Always aft over the side for any unfortunate person who may have fallen or throw in. The ships prop kicked up a rooster tail of a wave and behind the ship was a dazzling blue highway of phytoplankton. So, it was possible if someone fell, they might get spotted. The aft deck at night was reserved for the pot smokers on the ship and there was an unwritten rule for officers to avoid this area or face some difficulties. I tended to head up and to the center of the ship where alone I could sing sad songs of love gone wrong and get lost in the stars.

On the bridge the captain kept a big orange canvas man named Oscar. Oscar could not swim but was a great floater. At times, the captain would get angry with Oscar and throw him over the side.

You could be sleeping or watching a movie when he does this! Over the PA system they would blast, "This is a drill, this is a drill. Man Overboard! Man Overboard! Man, your stations. This is a drill." And of course we would all run around to our Stations, be accounted for, and everyone would search that dark rough water for poor Oscar. The ship would drop flares and then spin in a large fast circle to try and return to the spot where Oscar had been thrown in. Search lights would be switched on by the Signal Men, and the beams would cut across the water. It was always a race and the captain always with his stopwatch would time us. Now, he wanted Oscar back. Of course, the real training was to save one of us should we ever slip or get tossed in. Hypothermia was the fear of freezing to death in a short amount of time. But my fear would be those monster sharks that followed the ship day and night. Eating our garbage. Nightmare stuff for sailors.

At Seven in the morning," Reville, Reville, all hands heave out! The smoking lamp is lit." and that was our alarm clock. Always a mad dash to shower and shave, dress and run down to the mess deck for breakfast. On this ship breakfast was awesome. Eggs cooked your way, bacon, sausages, toast, bagels, donuts, fruit, cereals, oatmeal, milk, OJ, coffee and fresh  Bug Juice.

I was raised a poor kid and never saw food like that. I think the Navy could have been my calling. If I had stayed in, I might weigh about three hundred pounds by now. Lunch was always a variety of items to choose from, all delicious, but dinner on this navel vessel was like going to a combination of five-star restaurants. Nobody went hungry and nobody lost weight.

It might surprise you, but we had mail on the ships. Mail would be flown out to the Aircraft carrier in your task group, and they would helo it out to the surface fleet. Sometimes they would Hi-line the mail across from a larger ship, along with supplies. One day I got hi-lined to a ship to do some safe work. Once and never again, when the ships roll toward each other the line goes slack and if you are lucky enough to be sitting in that 'bosun chair,' well the saltwater comes rushing up and you get very wet. Of course, when the ships roll back you come flying out of the ocean like a happy dolphin on a tight string. Cold, scary, exciting, and I repeat never again.

Ports of Call are so exotic and exciting. This does depend on your attitude and sense of adventure because most of the ports are not your typical cruise ship destinations. After ten days of crossing the Atlantic, passing through six time zones and umpteenth sea drills from fire to nuclear attack drills we ended up in Rota Spain as our first stop. From there we made our way around Portugal and to the straights of Gibraltar. The second stop was to be Beaulieu France at the foot of the Maritime Alps. Tall mountains that fell into a dark blue Mediterranean Sea.

Dropping anchor, it went deep into the sea Hundreds of feet to hold our ship steady. The captain allowed one hour of swim call, after posting Gunner mates with rifles, just in case some sharks should join us. We had a blast jumping from the ship and climbing the cargo net to get back on board. The water was extremely cold and yet invigorating and refreshing. From shore dozens of small boats and paddle boats came out to see the Navy ship, and most were managed by French girls in topless bikinis. For a ship full of young sailors, it created a lot of cheering and waving by the crew.

Exotic ports of call, from Africa to Europe was the biggest benefit to military service and I will add a few stories of some of my favorite 'pit stops.' After six months of a Mediterranean cruise, it was time to return home, and every man looked forward to that. Gibraltar at the tip of Spain was to be our last port of call before we would make our run for the good old US of A. Gibraltar was under English rule, and English lads at pubs all had two things in common. They loved to drink, and loved to fight.

As our ship the 'USS Blakely' lay moored in the shadow of Gibraltar and sailors granted shore leave, some of us explored the honey-combed network of caves in the 'Rock'. But the big rock was the domain of some very wiley monkeys. They were a band of thieves of the highest caliber and very adept pickpockets. I would have loved to find where the monkeys kept their loot, I could have make a fortune.

After a few days the time came where we left .The Rock of Gibraltra' and the wooden piers behind. As watch was set for sea, We were called to Port of Arms on the deck of the ship. We lined up in dress uniform as we sailed out of the strait of Gibraltar into the tempestuous Atlantic Ocean. We 'saluted' the incoming Vessel with the exchange of duty and our captain blasted over the PA system, for both ships to hear, "I'm your Captain" by Grand Funk Railroad. As the two ships slid past each other in the waning sun, I realized, 'It was a glorious day.'

# Chapter 10

# Italians in Italy

Genoa

The USS Blakey had been out to sea for over a month patrolling deep waters off the African coast, running our drills and formations with the Med Pac fleet. The captain in the morning brief gave the promise of a Port stop in the Northern part of Italy, the armpit of Italy, and it sounded divine. It was now October, and the weather had turned damp and cold. The days were shrinking with less sunlight to work with. We steamed for a few days and nights and finally reached our Liberty port.

It was the port of Genoa in Italy, and as the ship lay too, alongside a dirty pier, on a dark damp rainy day, I was looking forward to spending the next few days of Liberty off the ship. I needed air, I needed space, and I needed to be far from anyone reassembling sailors or Navy.

Walking Genoa, Italy in the damp chill air I kept my Pea Coat buttoned tight, with the collar up over the back of my neck. It was October in the northern old country, my eyes darted here and there, taking in the shops with lit windows of myriad items for sale. Smoked escaped from the clay chimneys that grew from the rooftops. They looked warm and inviting these shops, but my mind was more into adventure, not shopping.

Finding the train station in the middle of town I followed my impulse to ride. Trains always led to adventure, and I purchased a ticket to head South on the next one out. It was a uneventful ride and after a couple of hours the train pulled into Livorno, just outside of Pisa. I had spent some time here in the Summer and it was memorable. I jumped off and headed to a local tavern, the weather had warmed up, and a cold beer did sound good about now. The contest of throwing darts with locals and watching two big guys laughing and finger wrestling was cool until one guy broke the other guy's finger, and the bone came poking out. I kept the beer down but that was a sign to move on.

I was getting a bit tipsy and decided to find refuge in a genuinely charming hotel in town. Entering the room, it was spacious and first class, but I was really confused with the two-porcelain bowls in the bathroom. His and Hers? Why did 'Hers' have a water fountain in the center of the bowl? I Finally figured it was one of those Bidets that rich people always had in their bathrooms. Never had seen one. When I tried to flush it, the water shot up and sprayed me in the face. Damn those rich people and their crazy ideas.

Must have fallen asleep because the next day I awoke with a pounding head and queasy feeling in my gut. But it was time to get moving so I showered and dressed. Wanting to start to head back I could not afford to miss ships movement, a court martial offense. Plus, not sure I wanted to spend the rest of my life here in Livorno.

Taking stock of my situation, I realized my pockets were now empty. I would have sworn I had saved enough cash to return, maybe a thief in the hotel while I slept? My thoughts grew cold, my heart kind of missed a beat. Oh No! How was I going to get back to Genoa, and to my fair ship the USS Blakely 1072, without money for the train, I became worried and desperate.

Now I never figured out what happened, was I robbed by the bell hop after passing out in the room? Or did I drink the money away, leaving only enough for the hotel room. That really did not matter right now because this was chaos time. Leaving the hotel, I walked down to the boarded-up Cafes on the water and watched the seagulls circle overhead. Beach furniture piled high on the boardwalk the chilled wind blew in long gust blowing sand up into my face. I was despondent and left with only one option.

I clasped my hands together and prayed to God. "God, please help me get out of this mess. I need your help and have nowhere else to turn." Out of the corner of my eye I saw some pretty pink paper blowing in the breeze. It came to rest at my feet and when my eyes focused from behind my clenched fingers, I saw a 10,000 Lira note. "Thank you, God." I cried out and then jumped on it with all four feet.

Now in those days the exchange rate was about seven hundred Lira to a dollar, so I was not rich, but I was saved. I had enough for that ticket. I ran to the train station, after much discussion and waving of hands I got a ticket back to Genoa. I was lucky to catch a train north, just pulling out. I took a seat in a wooden cubicle with two wooded benches facing each other on the train. Soon I was joined by a large Italian family with a dozen kids, parents and grandma. It was a fascinating ride, those few hours north. What with little ones climbing all over me and asking endless questions in Italian that I would never understand, over the noise of the train. Grandma sitting across from me, with deep brown eyes piercing my thoughts kept feeding me chucks of bread and cheese, dried fruits and non-stop talking in

Italian. My occasional nod and my one Italian word, "Prego" kept her talking for hours and the food flowing. It was delightful.

It felt good to be back on the ship, happy to have survived my adventure. Thankful for Grandma and the Italian family for showing me the hearts of the common Italians, and for God, who had rescued me once again.

# Chapter 11
# North Africa

TUNIS

It was the time of Ramadan, the holiest of Holy days for the Muslims, and I found myself in Tunis, Tunisia. A Muslim state, at the top of Africa filled with sand and camels. Now Tunis is the capital and quite large metropolis with many tall buildings. As I walked the streets there was no noise or cars on the street, no people, and so quiet that even street dogs tip toed from garbage can to garbage can.

It was early AM, and I went back to the ship, the USS Blakely and waited for the Ambassador's Limo to roll down the dock and pick me and a few buddies up. He had been so kind as to invite a group of sailors for a late lunch. Since the city was dead, I sure didn't want to miss a free meal.

The Ambassador's home blended right into the desert, and after a brief tour we settled around a large table on the veranda overlooking the desert dunes. The fine sand blowing off the top of the dunes reminded me of stinging sea mist; the desert was an ocean of sand. After some delightful stories lunch was served on an open-air pavilion. What a treat!  A huge pyramid shaped mound of Couscous, my first time with Couscous, with little chicken legs and broccoli poking out.

We were sailors and we ate like sailors that had been lost at sea for weeks. The cold beer chased all those little chicken legs down our throats till we were bloated with food. Now our dessert was chilled melons and assorted fruits. The Ambassador warned us to use the little forks and knives and not to touch the skins. "The skin of the fruit is covered with deadly pesticides," he claimed. "It worked well on insects, and careless sailors."

I mentioned how quiet Tunis was when I had ventured out onto its streets that morning. The ambassador told me to come back after dark, It will be a different city and there would be more people on the streets. You may be pleasantly surprised.

More people was a miscalculation by the ambassador. When the sun went down doors were flung wide open and everyone and everything came out into the streets. Women ran back and forth with large trays of bread and pastries balanced on their covered heads. Charcoal fires were burning on every corner with meaty Shika bobs and cherry tomatoes. Food, People, and that funky Muslim music filled the night. Old men with large hookahs sat in doorways with large blue clouds of smoke swirling around them.

I was right in the middle of them dancing, laughing, singing, and living life. What fun.

The next day I awoke and was once again ready to explore this hot city with no trees or even a breeze. Ramadan was over and the streets were filled, like most big cities, with hustle and bustle. My friend Lew and I requested permission to go ashore and was granted permission from the office of the deck. We made our way down the dock into the heat of the city, and into the heart of the old city, Narrow streets of stone, the bazzars and tiny shops were right out of a movie. We spent hours roaming the streets and narrow alleys. It really was a foreign land. Down one narrow alley we found a quaint shop where I spotted two beautiful full-length robes of white with gold trim. Oh, I wanted them. I started negotiating with the shop owner, and I realized I was going to need my best bartering skills, he was one tough cookie. I was going to have to shift my gears and get creative.

I turned to the shop owner and showed him the newest Kodak Camera on the market. I just happen to have it in the factory box with all the paperwork in my possession. I saw the pupils of his eyes dilate and nostrils flare, ever so slightly, and I was sure I had him, and he was sure he had me. We negotiated some more and finally I threw in ten dollars if his wife would be kind enough to wrap both robes in brown parchment for me.

Now a little side note: When I was in Florence, Italy, I had visited the leaning tower of Pisa. From the top of the tower, I had leaned over the rail and dropped this very same camera. It was a tremendous blow to me and the camera, and it took many nights for me to glue it all together. It looked good but it would never work again. Putting it back in the box I hoped to find a use for it someday.

Lew and I, walked out of the shop and got a few feet down the cobble stones when the shop owner ran out and said, "wait! let me get a picture of you two guys." I knew this was not going to end well, and as the shop owner removed the camera from the box, then aiming it at us, he pushed the button. The camera fell apart in pieces!

I was already yelling at Lew to run. And running is what we did.

The shop owner recovered quickly from my deceit and grabbed a long-wooded pole, he set off in pursuit behind us. He was yelling in Arabic, angry Arabic, and soon others joined in the pursuit. Lew and I ran with the fear of what would happen if they caught us, and glancing back I could see the number had grown to about fifteen men with various weapons to inflict bodily harm. Me holding the package as if it was a football we dashed through the narrow streets and alleys, across the modern roads and sidewalks of Tunis, we had a final dash down the long wooden pier and a quick burst up the gang plank. "Request permission to come aboard" we yelled out and the OOD said, "make it so." We ran to hide in the electronic shop, glancing over the side before we hid ourselves, we could see the angry mob, yelling and marching on the wooden pier the ship was tied to. The Quarter Deck had men with automatic weapons, so the mob did not dare to board and search for us.

Later the Captain would call me into his stateroom and ask me what the hell did I do this time? And after explaining, he said "wouldn't you like to just return that package so we can avoid an international incident?" I told the captain, "No, I don't think so. The guy was trying to screw me with some lame deal, and I just got the better of him."

The captain with a sigh of registration restricted me to the ship, claiming it was safer for everyone. I never went back out into Tunisa, the next night we set sail for Augusta Bay, Sicily.

My next big adventure.

# Chapter 12
# Locksmith 2.0

Locksmith 2.0

As a locksmith for most of my adult life, I have enjoyed many distinct aspects of the trade. My greatest joy in locksmithing, for me, has always been opening stuff. At an early age, opening cars and opening trunks of cars was my introduction to locksmithing 2.0. I have had moments working for the police when "popping" the trunk of a vehicle might reveal a dead body, [horrible smell] or money, drugs, or one time a portable Meth lab [horrible smell].

Later in life, safe work became a staple of income for me, and the challenge of opening a locked steel box with a complicated lock designed to keep people like me out was the ultimate test of skill. Finding the 'sweet spot' to drill and open a 'box,' could give me migraine headache. Sometimes hours with a borescope peeking thru a ¼" drilled hole through hard plate and spinning a dial to line up wheels in an exact configuration, always in a cramped location like a closet or bathroom, was my definition of time well spent. When everything finally lined up and the bolt handle suddenly turned, what an adrenaline rush. You could jump to your feet screaming, "Yeah

Baby! I beat you! Na nah na nah nah!" Peeking inside was always fun, but the "opening" was always the real thrill.

As my career progressed, I moved more into commercial work and reached a point where I left the lucrative field of automotive lock-smithing behind. I found myself doing bank work and the world of safe deposit boxes was a big part of it. Safe deposit boxes have always been fun to open, sometimes challenging because of all the assorted designs and manufacturers of the locks. For the uninformed layper-son, a safe deposit lock is two locks in one metal casing mounted to the door. Two different keys are required to open it, one owned by the bank, called a 'guard key,' the other owned by the bank customer, called the 'renter's key.' Opening safe deposit boxes are preformed for either a bank client who has lost his keys or for the bank. For the bank it is done usually once a year where you come in and drill several boxes that have been abandoned by clients for several reasons. Sometimes people forget they have boxes and neglect to make the yearly rental fee. Letters go out and phone calls are attempted, but if the client cannot be reached after a period of time, boxes are drilled. Sometimes people die leaving behind a box empty or filled with valuables. After a period of time, the bank will drill the box.

Every state has certain laws and procedures to follow; most will require one or more witnesses and a notary to be present. And of course, I was the locksmith of choice to drill the box. A quick note, I use the word drill, and in the old days we drilled for the screws holding the lock to the door. In this modern world we now have specialized tools that pick or manipulate the locks open. This is cleaner and more professional. People are sometimes disappointed to not see me pull out a big drill, hammer, and crowbars.

In this chapter I want to touch on two safe deposit box drillings, maybe three, that stick out in my memory. Every locksmith has comparable stories. Once had a friend that drilled a box in Georgia, and he found a rough draft of the constitution. So, my tales may sound wild, but these things happen quite frequently.

I drilled a large box once for a bank down on the beach. It was going to be one of two boxes rented by the same man and drilled for non-payment that had spanned two years. Upon opening the first box we discovered it was filled with cash. Counting the bills for the audit, it came to roughly sixty-eight thousand dollars. The branch manager seeing so much cash double checked the name on the contract and realized it was the owner of the Italian restaurant just blocks away. She called the man, who must of ran all the way from his business, to claim his cash and to open and remove another considerable sum from the second box. Red-faced he quietly explained that he had forgotten all about this money he had 'squirreled' away. I believed it was money he had 'skimmed' off the restaurant to avoid taxes and possibly sharing with a partner. I was amazed that there are people that could forget about large sums of cash like that.

In the late eighties I drilled a small safe deposit box for a bank in Fort Lauderdale. Standing there with three ladies we opened the box to find numerous photos of couples involved in sexual intercourse. Under the photos was a device which at first seemed confusing, but with the device there were instructions, which explained the device was a 'penis enlargement tool.' The women were gagging and screaming over this sicko and his toy.

You see, banks have little private rooms for customers to go sit and view the contents of the safe deposit boxes. They are allowed to take their box to these rooms to load or empty in private. Obviously, this sicko was using the room, determined after checking the sign in logs, twice a week to become 'more of a man.' I still laugh recalling how difficult a time it was for the ladies to do the inventory descriptions, a detailed report required by law when drilling unclaimed boxes.

My third and last story is about drilling a box that was ten by ten by twenty-four inches deep. The lock opened easily enough and opening the door I went to remove the 'tin,' what you might call the box, and it just would not budge. I enlisted some help from one of the three women in the vault with me, and it slid out and onto the floor. Opening the lid and looking inside we, all three, skipped a heartbeat. It was filled to the top with a South African coin referred to as a Gold Krugerrand. Each Krugerrand had a weight of one ounce, with a purity of about 97 percent twenty-two karat gold. Each coin in 1995 had a value of about Four hundred US dollars. We counted over fifteen thousand coins, and I estimated the value at over six million. That was 1995 today's estimated value would top out at over 35,000,000 US dollars. What a haul for an unclaimed bank vault box.

Now this is where the story turns weird. On top of this was a letter, and the letter was addressed to the man's wife. It has been thirty years since that day so I cannot quote exactly the letter, but the heart and flow of the letter are as follows.

"Dear Sweetheart," it starts out. "If you are reading this letter, then we can assume I am dead, and you have opened my safe deposit box. Inside, as you can see there is a great deal of gold Krugerrands. Darling, I want you to come to the bank on Christmas, our anniversaries, your birthday, and remove a gold coin. Cash it in and buy yourself something nice. Remember I love you, your Husband." After reading the letter I turned around, and all three women were crying. "What a Man" one of them said.

It could have been a great love story, but life can be cruel, and in this story that is what happens. As an unclaimed box with no legitimate person claiming ownership, all property becomes property of the state. The wife never saw a gold Krugerrand. Yet, I am sure the state of Florida put the money to beneficial use.

# Chapter 13

# Big Blue

'**B**ig Blue'

I entered a short story essay contest back in August 2000, in a national locksmith trade publication, The Locksmith Ledger, sponsored by Lock Masters and the legendary Mark Miller. It had to be on tools, and the grand prize was 5,000 dollars in locksmith tools. I had never shared anything I wrote with anyone, so I had no expectations when I entered a small piece from one of my experiences. Imagine my surprise when I took first prize. I felt like a peacock with lots of pretty feathers. It has been twenty-five years, and I am going to reprint it here. I hope you enjoy reading this as much as I did in writing it.

My Boss was terribly upset with me back in February of 1992 when I presented her with an invoice in the amount of, 169.79 for a new drill motor. It was a one third horsepower, half inch drill chuck, with reversible and variable speed, double insulated, Blue Makita drill motor and carrying case.

"But boss" I whined in my most defensive voice, "you told me to go out and buy a new drill to replace my burned-out antique of a machine." "Yeah, yeah!" she replied, "but not the Maserati of drill motors. You will have me in the poor house before the end of the month." She did finally agree to reimburse me $169.79, and as I ran out the door, I could hear her yell, "No more spending sprees for you. You are cut off!"

I soon learned to love that Blue Makita Drill Motor. It went everywhere with me, even home with me at night, where I would tuck it in its toolbox for a good night's rest. There was no door, nor frame or lock that we could not master. We were invincible as job after job would pour in, and we would knock 'em out of the park. What a team Big Blue and I were becoming until one sweltering day in July of 1996 an unusual call came in. The job was for one of the Airline's freight offices on the Airport Tarmac I was to install a heavy-duty lock on a heavy gauge steel door with steel and concrete filled frame. Now I have done this type of work a hundred times before. But this time the job gave me the 'Willys' and I felt like something was going to go wrong.

Arriving at the Airport, Big Blue and I approached the job with our usual determination. We laid the power cords out on the tarmac with our tools and lock. The work was going well and soon I had prepped all the holes in the door and frame. I dropped Big Blue to the Tarmac seven or eight feet behind me and began assembling the lock on the door.

Minutes went by as I intently focused on my task when suddenly there was a horrible high-pitched screech from behind! Fear gripped my spine and adrenaline raced through my body. My Stanley Phillips screwdriver flew from my hand to the asphalt, and I threw myself into the freight doorway and into the freight bay. A second later a yellow two-ton Toyota forklift plowed it's two forks into the wall and frame where I had just been standing.

As I slowly stood, visibly shaken, I asked myself, that noise, it saved my life. What made it?' I looked from the doorway to the yellow forklift, and a young driver was rubbing sleep from his eyes. Big Blue was wedged under one of the six-foot tires. My one third horsepower, half inch chuck, variable speed, reversible, double insulated, blue Makita was wedged under one of those six-foot tires! It had wedged there with a long scream warning me and giving me time to toss myself out of harm's way. I begged the driver to move his rig back off my drill motor with tears in my eyes.

Big Blue, the top was covered in black rubber skid marks, and the bottom had an asphalt tattoo. Would she ever work again, I asked myself. Plugging it in, I held it in my hands, gently squeezing the trigger. It was sluggish at first, then it spit out a few pebbles and began to work smoothly. I assessed the variable speed and then the reverse, everything was fine.

That evening when I returned to the shop, I repeated the events of the day to my boss. She looked up at me, after hearing my tale and said, "you see Ray, there is value in buying the best. And it saved your life!"

When I tell this story someone always ask, "what happen to Big Blue?" A few years later a thief broke into my service truck and made off with some tools and 'Big Blue.' I still miss that drill, I only hope she ended up in a lovely home.

# Chapter 14

# Jamaican Locksmith

Jamaican Locksmith

In 1973 I joined the Military Service; to be specific, I joined the US Navy. I begged for, and was evaluated at recruitment for electronic school, one of the toughest classes at that time in the US Navy. At the completion of bootcamp I was allowed to enter Electronics School, taught at the Great Lakes Navel facility outside of Chicago, Illinois. A real feather in my hat considering I had not finished high school. The classes were difficult, heavy in Math and Algebra. I had to attend night school for algebra, to be able to grasp the concepts and theories, but I loved the material and soaked it up like a sponge.

Having been a locksmith for three plus years I saw the future in security, and it was going to require heavy electronic skills. Mechanical ability would not be enough, and it was only a matter of time before keys and locks would evolve into the digital world. Back in the sixties there were no electronic locks, no elaborate complexity to security. Life was a lot simpler, but I knew strange and new things were coming.

Graduating "A" school in the Great Lakes area outside of Chicago, I was sent to my duty station. It is funny that before you leave school, you fill out a dream sheet where you list three places you would like to be assigned. The Navy carefully considers this before assigning your final destination. Key West, Hawaii, or San Diego were my choices. As you can guess no one ever gets their dream sheet pick, and I was sent to Charleston, South Carolina. "Agah!" I cried. My mind filled with images of dusty dirt roads through endless fields of dark green tobacco and cotton fields. Southerners in overalls and pretty farm girls all missing a front tooth. I always was a city boy, big time big city. I cried when I read my orders, but there was no going back. Charleston, South Carolina, I was on my way.

Actually, I was stationed on a ship, The USS Blakely DE1072, home ported out of Charleston. It was in Dry Dock at the time, and after asking "permission to come aboard" at the quarter deck, I discovered a loud, noisy, dirty, ship getting retrofitted. I spent my first three months on this ship 'mess cooking' in a hot galley. Spare time was spent standing fire watch over shipyard welders burning holes in metal and asbestos covered pipes, hoping they would not set the ship a blaze. Exploring the ship and discovering all the tricks and customs of shipboard life rounded out those first three months.

After a scorching summer, the time came when the ship finally moved out of the dry dock and into the Cooper River, where ships belong. Tied to "Q" dock at the navy base, I was allowed to finally leave the galley and entered the domain of the electronic techs, a large room on the main deck referred to as the 'ET Shack.' It was the lair of a brotherhood of men, who talked electrons, resistors, and football. My new home for the next three and a half years.

The 'Blakely' left her moorings at "Q" dock one late afternoon and began a steady journey down the Cooper River and through a channel lined on both sides with massive granite boulders. Working below deck on a UHF radio, I noticed the room was swaying side to side as the ship made her way to open sea. My brain tried to make sense of the motion and suddenly I was nauseous. I made a mad run up and out to the railings to heave my lunch and my breakfast over the side. This was the one and only time I ever got seasick. Thank you, God. Focusing on the horizon helped and soon I was feeling better, yet I remained topside enjoying the color of the ocean turning from brown to green to dark blue.

Passing the channel buoy, Two Charlie, the ship turned south by southeast and headed for deep water and my first port of call, Guantanamo, Cuba. Gitmo was our name for that special slice of hell down there. No trees, no grass, extra heat, and sunshine. It was a training ground for East coast ships and their captains. We would run drills from sunrise to late at night for any and all scenarios. Fire training, nuclear attacks to missile launches. Man-overboard drills, to calls at all hours, "General Quarters! General Quarters! Man, your battle stations!"

After four weeks of intense training, we got a reprieve. The ship's crew made its way down to a secluded beach and ballfield on Gitmo, for some well-deserved R & R. The cooks set up large grills, hamburgers and hotdogs were cooked then served on toasted buns with chips and all kinds of side dishes. Ice chest appeared with icy cold Budweiser and music of the seventies reverberated in the air. The camaraderie was open and honest among our fellow shipmates. It was a rare and special time.

The small beach, staffed by two tanned lifeguards nervously watched over drunk sailors enjoying the salt water. I wanted to snorkel out past the rope buoys to explore, but the guards would not have any of that. I suspected the deeper water would hide Conchs, a prized shell and delicious meat for chowders and salads. I decided I would return the next morning before the lifeguards assumed their duties and explore these deeper waters.

Early the next morning I ran to the beach, at the water's edge I donned my mask and fins, plunging right in. Swimming quietly out past the floating buoys in the early morning sun I was soon floating over a bed of seagrass in crystal clear water. Ideal for conchs and it was not long before I found a couple large shells on the move. Swimming down twenty to thirty feet of water I snatched the shells off the sea floor and shoved them in a catch bag. A beautiful red starfish joined my plunder.

As I started my slow ascent to the surface three Black Tip sharks suddenly appeared in my field of vision. Six or seven feet in length, they came remarkably close and circled as my snorkel broke the surface of the water. I had a quick tinge of fear but fought down the urge to turn and swim like hell for the shore. That would spell disaster for the sharks sensing my fear would have chased me down and eaten me. They looked very hungry.

Staying calm, I slowly backed my way to the beach, always keeping my eyes on the trio. They did the same to me, keeping me in their field of vision looking for a weakness, escorting me to the shallows.

Exiting the water, I noticed the lifeguards had come on duty. They came running up to me and seeing the bag with Conchs started yelling, telling me that I had broken the rules by swimming so far out and before the official start time. In a loud voice I was told that I was not allowed to go to their beach or swim in the water for the rest of the week. It was to leave immediately.

All I could think of was to say, "Thank you" with a big smile, leaving two lifeguards with puzzled expressions on their faces.

Four more grueling weeks was spent in Cuban waters. We did get a short reprieve with a trip to Port Au Prince in Haiti. The city was packed with people, and everyone engaged in some type of commerce. I always loved exploring new lands and people alone. Most sailors headed for the bars, Not being a drinker, I would wander in solitude among the vast crowds of humanity.

I found a large open-air market, looking for a souvenir, I pushed my way into the heart of the crowd, a sea of brown faces. At a stand I saw some well-made straw hats of stylish design. I tried a few on and finally decided on a nifty, small brimmed, hat. "How much?" I asked. A young man replied, "two dollars." What a deal.

I pulled a fifty-dollar bill from my pocket, the only money I had, and started to ask if he could make change. Someone from behind reached up and snatched the bill from my hand. He was off running through the crowd. I could not give chase because the man was a brown face in a sea of brown faces and the crush of bodies too much. I had just lost fifty dollars and was feeling low. I turned and started to walk away, after a few moments of disbelief over what had happened. As I pushed through the crowd a young man grabbed my arm. I turned and with a big smile on the young man he said, "Sir, you forgot your hat. And here is your change, Forty-eight dollars."

In a land of strangers, I found the definition of honesty.

The ship headed to Puerto Rico, and we made Port at Roosevelt Roads. In the seventies it was a dock surrounded by a jungle and mountains. The days were spent target practicing with the ship's big gun, the fifty-four-millimeter cannon on the forward deck. On a small island, Vieques off the coast of Puerto Rico, we bombarded with shells and an occasional missile day after day and into the night. Later in life I would meet an individual that claimed to live in a small village on the opposite side of that island. I cannot fathom what it was like growing up in the backyard of a Navel bombing site. I did notice his hearing sucked.

We moored alongside a Royal Navy Frigate in Roosevelt Roads, and boys being boys our crew challenged the English crew to a game of football. European style, Their rules. I volunteered to play not knowing what I was getting myself into. We all made our way to possibly the only level playing field on that side of the island and setting up goals and boundaries we went at it. The English kicked our butts and at one point we poor American sailors had to forfeit or die. Sorry Uncle Sam, it was a pathetic display. Never ran so much.

The unseen benefit to the football game, was that the English, had bars on their military ships. We were all invited back to drink english ale on their vessel and celebrate in our 'mates' victory.

I and three of my navy friends rented a car one night while in Puerto Rico to cruise the island. We were having a marvelous time drinking and telling tall tales when out on a desolate highway the car overheated. Steam escaped from under the hood and when we poured water into the radiator it would flow out through some mystery holes in the coolant system. It was late after midnight, and we needed to return to the ship. I saw a house up the road on a hill and decided to see if I could find some help. Knocking on the door an old Spanish man confronted me at the entrance.

I was polite and explained the situation, pleading for some help. "Uno momento por favor." The old man said, and he left me standing at the door. When he returned, he held out his hand, giving me two brown speckled eggs. I wanted to say, "sorry I'm not hungry" but he quickly added, "you go fix car with eggs. Put eggs in Radiator and drive home. Buenos Nochtas" and he slammed the door in my face.

Wow, I thought how weird that was. My friends, becoming desperate, asked if I had found help, and I explained what had transpired.

We took a vote, and we all agreed to crack the eggs and drop them in the radiator. Adding water, we returned the cap to the radiator and slammed the hood. Starting the car, we began our trip back to the ship, all eyes on the temperature gauge. To our delight and surprise the temperature started coming down and soon we were cruising with no worries and no steam.

I believe what happened was the egg made its way to the holes in the coolant system and on its journey cooked then jammed in the radiator holes, preventing the leaks as a cooked rubbery substance. The old man had saved the day with some island ingenuity.

Finishing our gunnery practice in Puerto Rico we headed to Ocho Rios, Jamaica for some serious R & R. This was the Seventies, and the island was beautiful. After weeks at sea when we approached the island the smell of flowers and trees was in the air long before we saw the island, a green mountain rising from the Caribbean sea. Docking in a protective cove, Liberty was granted for all personnel except those that stood the watch. I and a group of sailors headed to Dunn's falls, a speculator river and waterfall that fell from the mountain tops into the sea.

At the bottom of the falls was a changing station where, as a group, we rented a locker to store our clothes. We donned bathing suits and then sprinted into the water. Icy chilly water it was, but it was summer and delightful to climb and splash our way to the top and then slide and climb back down.

Returning to the changing station a few hours later we realized that we had lost the key to the locker, in the river. There was no way we could go back and find the key, so we turned to the attendant and asked for solutions. "No!" he said when we asked if he had a spare key, and desperation was starting to set in as we stood there in bathing shorts dripping wet. "Mon, you need a locksmith, do I call one for you?"

the attendant offered. "Yes, please." We all answered. Fifteen minutes later a young Jamaican man with the long 'dread Locks' showed up. "Which one, Mon, he politely asked." and we quickly escorted him to the locker.

Looking at us, he stated his fee, which we agreed to pay, and then he asked us to stand back and give him some space. Reaching down into a long toolbox he carried, he removed a long, razor-sharp machete. Raising it above his head, he attacked the locker with vigor and several vicious blows. Chunks of wood and splinters flew in the air and in minutes our locker was opened. This was my introduction to a Jamaican Locksmith.

That night in Ocho's Rios, some of my fellow crewmates approached me and asked if I could help them to obtain some 'Reefer.' I had a reputation for being a negotiator on the USS Blakely, and truthfully, I enjoyed the art of 'Barter.' The thought of going head-to-head with the local culture appealed to my ego and I agreed.

It is not hard to find Jamaicans selling pot on this island, and on a hotel balcony looking out over the ocean we were approached by one such individual. Negotiating with this young man was tough and he wanted to sell the group a joint for one dollar. I laughed at that and replied, "Yes, in the states that might be a good deal, but we are here in Jamaica. The stuff grows wild! I know you just go up the hill and pick it. We want five joints for a dollar and that is our offer." I said definitely.

He was a little upset, and finally we agreed on a simple solution. "Okay, Mon" he said, "Let us smoke one joint here for one dollar. If you still want the other four, I will sell them to you for a second dollar." "Agreed." I replied and we all sat down in a circle to sample the 'wacky tobacco.'

The young man pulled out a sheet of hotel stationary, nine inches by eleven inches, and laid out a healthy amount of marijuana on the paper. Quickly and with adept fingers he rolled the paper into the longest and fattest joint in the history of the world. Lighting this creation was difficult, the sailors passed it among themselves, occasionally hacking and coughing. It would sputter out at times, and the Jamaican would laugh and relight the joint. Time may have stood still as the sun just set on the horizon defying to sink into the sea. The sailors one at a time fell to their sides in fits of laughter and incoherent babbling. What little was left of that first joint was tossed to the waves below the patio.

The Jamaican turned to me, with a handful of hotel stationary and asked, "Mon, are you ready for the other four numbers?" "Oh, Hell No!" And I gave him his five dollars.

# Chapter 15

# Family

F amily

They say you cannot pick your family, but if you could I am sure I would be a 'only' child. Brothers, sisters, children, even parents can be a source of embarrassment, leaving you red-faced at times. In writing, it is said you must include the good, the bad, and the ugly! Family stories, I believe, can contain all three. With that being said, I will tell only a few of my favorites.

My brother Randy was a wild and crazy guy. He was the closest to me in personality, always pushing the envelope, never worried what others might think or say. Randy was thin of build with a dark moustache below a thin nose and narrow set eyes. His shirts had no sleeves, his transportation was a chopper, and he affiliated with some motorcycle gang in South Florida. Somewhere on his body you could always find a pistol of high caliber.

Randy owned a little boat that was flat bottomed and powered by a 25 horsepower Honda motor. He would love to go down to the Florida Keys with his boat and skim over the grass beds into deeper blue water. Dropping anchor, he would don scuba gear and slip over the side. Swimming some distance, he would raid lobster pots set by hard working fishermen. Winter months he would target stone crab traps. This was a good way to get shot in the Florida Keys, but he managed to avoid injury.

Early one weekday morning, he drove to the keys and inserted his boat at a secluded boat ramp into the sea. Cranking the motor, he pushed off the dock and across shallow water passing just above the seagrass covered floor.

With a twist of the throttle, he held the tiller and guided his boat out of the Mangroves, and then out to sea. The heavy fog that rolled in during the night was starting to dissipate and the flat green sea held the promise of adventure. He felt confident he was going to have a good day catching fish, maybe raiding some traps.

About forty-five minutes out of the mangroves and into deeper water, the sea turned dark blue. Randy felt this could be the spot, cutting the engine, left him in complete silence, he dropped two lines with hooks and live bait into the briny depth. The eerier fog was heavy, a tall white wall encircling his boat, he would need it to burn off to find his way back, but for now peace and solitude were medicine for his soul.

The hum of a twin-engine aircraft cut into the fog from the south and quickly grew into a growing roar. From the sound he knew the plane was flying low just above the fog and instinctively he crouched down into the hull. No reason to lose his head to a lost aircraft. The noise grew very close, and then he saw the airplane, a single engine Beechcraft plowing a furrow into the fog bank with its spinning prop.

There was a large splash as the plane passed overhead, a large bundle had fallen from the plane into the sea, spraying him with sea foam. Damn that was close he thought. He strained to see what had fallen off the plane, only meters from his position. Much to his surprise he saw a large square package wrapped in green canvas floating off his starboard bow.

In his heart he knew what it was, but he had to go and make sure. The little motor came to life as he pulled the cord, the rod and reels quickly reeled up, secured and put away. He took control of the tiller and slowly made his way to the floating package.

Nervous and excited, he reached for the package and almost swamping the boat as he pulled it aboard. With the motor in idle he began his inspection. Cutting open one corner of the package, the heady green smell of fresh marijuana almost made him faint with thrill and excitement.

His mind raced with "What to do?" Thoughts of selling this stash and having all this money ran through his mind. Never having ever been Lucky, he was intoxicated with his discovery. He knew his time had finally come.

The fog was lifting and fear of being discovered by the smugglers or Coast Guard forced him into action. Hiding his find under a small tarp, he turned his boat towards the mainland and opened the throttle all the way. Quickly he made his way back to the Mangroves and boat ramp.

At shore he sprang from the boat and quickly ran to his old Ford van and two wheeled boat trailer.

Backing hazardously into the water to retrieve his vessel, his heart pounding in his chest, His head spinning left and right, he looked guilty as hell. But no one was out this morning, no one was watching and he made a good clean get away. Driving the speed limit, unusual for Randy, he was careful all the way back to Miami. At his apartment he stowed his boat and moved his cargo to his van. He was finally able to breathe a sigh of relief.

Randy knew he would need to sell this to realize those heady dreams of fast cash. So, after cleaning up, he spent the day putting the word out on the street that he had some dynamite stuff to sell. Being in a motorcycle gang he did have some connections and buyers seemed to be lining up. It looked like in the next few days all his troubles would be over. Things were going so well that he decided to host a small celebration with his six brothers and two sisters and close friends. All were invited to come to his apartment to enjoy some refreshments and sample the best of the best.

Now aside from myself, my brothers and sisters all did show up for this party of parties. All came with spouses and most even brought their kids. The Iglesias Clan was a degenerate group and most saw no harm in smoking with their children. Laughter, happiness and good times reverberated in the smoke-filled rooms of Randy's apartment into the night.

I doubt anyone gave a second thought when there was a knock at the door. And I'm sure it took a few minutes for the three big guys with stocking masks and automatic weapons to step inside and get everyone's attention.

Now with a subdued atmosphere, the three big guys had put a damper on the festivities, The pot induced laughter dissipated into thin air, and cries of fear from some of the women replaced it.

They were put back-to-back and roughly tied together, children too. Of course, there were a few brothers with mouths they couldn't keep shut. Bravado in the face of automatic weapons, they got to feel the butt end of those rifles and losing consciousness they were a lot easier to tie up.

Randy was quarantined and was questioned harshly. He had to spill his guts that the good stuff, the large square bale was in his van downstairs. Politely asking him for his keys, he was hog tied but not blind folded. He watched as they took his TV and stereo, loading the equipment in the van, the Banditos left as hastily as they had arrived.

I guess it was late morning with much yelling before someone finally called the police to open the apartment and they were untied and released.  Randy was in shell shock after losing all his marijuana, van, TV and stereo. The van was later found, a burned-out shell in the Everglades. He was devasted. I guess he should have kept insurance on it.

Anyway, I guess the party was a huge success because the next day the sad story appeared in the Miami Herald along with a group photo of the family all bound and gagged. And to think that I missed out on all that fun.

Not sure why but children are considered family. At times they cause more pain than joy and yet we keep a special spot in our hearts for them. I have six children, and they all have given me grief and happy relief. They could fill up a book by themselves, but I will only include one tale here.

One of my children was allowed to use my baby blue Cadillac Coup de Ville for transport to work and school. One morning he woke, hungry and thirsty, and decided to make a run to the neighborhood convenience store. After buying a rather large soda and some donuts he adjusted the radio volume and set a course for home. A distance of three or four blocks. On the return trip, one of the donuts made an attempt to escape his fate and leaped from his lap onto the floorboard of the Cadillac. The driver, young and hungry, was having none of that, and was losing interest in the road, focused on the donut rolling across the floorboard. The donut was headed for the underside of the passenger seat, and the driver was now in full pursuit.

The car, left to its own devices, careened off the pavement at a low rate of speed. It traversed the grassy slope of a single-family home and came to a complete stop after crashing into a vintage, late sixties Mustang. The young man shaken, but with donut in hand, stepped from the Cadillac to see the damage. I'm sure his thoughts were, "Oh, my God!"

As he looked at the badly damaged Mustang and the damage inflicted on the Coupe de Ville. He did notice the lack of witnesses and quickly climbed back behind the wheel. He checked the level of his soda, virtually untouched and he cracked the car ignition back on.

As he backed out into the street, he noticed the car was not operating correctly. Placing the vehicle in park, he jumped out and walked around the car. The back right fender had been caved in crushing the tire and not allowing it to spin freely. Pulling madly on the rear quarter panel did little to help. "Got to escape", he must have thought, climbing back into the car he put it into 'drive' and gunned the engine. The car moved forward. He proceeded home to the squealing protest of the right rear tire.

In the driveway and back home he relaxed behind the wheel. Perhaps he closed his eyes and enjoyed the last bite of donut with his soda thinking, "Wow! Dodged a bullet."

As he climbed out of the Cadilliac his eyes went to the road where he saw, much to his dismay, a black heavy skid mark from the driveway off and down the road from where he had just come. Yes, the car had left a trail from the accident scene to home. Off in the distance could be heard police sirens. The only logical thing left to do was...... Run!

I got the call at work; it was my wife and there was hysteria in her voice. I had to ask her to slow down. "What do you mean you're making your one phone call? From the police station!" "Yes. Yes, I'll come right over."

The Mustang owner had watched the Cadillac drive off leaving a hideous skid mark on the road. Going out and seeing the Classic

Mustang no longer 'classy' he called the police. It must have been a detective that showed up on the accident scene, because they were able to follow the black skid mark from the Mustang to the Cadillac parked in my driveway.

The police had knocked on the door of the house and when my wife had opened the door they asked, "Is that your car in the driveway?"

"Of course it is!" she blurted out. "Then you are under arrest" the police said taking her into custody. She was read the Miranda rights and handcuffed.

Of course, all of this was straightened out, and at one point, an arrest warrant issued for the young man. Later he would be found hiding under a bridge and brought in for swift justice. After repairs made to both cars, life would slow back down to its steady family life crawl.

# Chapter 16
# Baseball

B aseball

At one point in the early 1990's, Wayne Huizenga established 'The Florida Marlins' as the newest franchise baseball team to compete in South Florida. What excitement swept through the community, after all Miami and Fort Lauderdale was heavy Latin, and Spanish speaking ball players were the predominate players in the sport. Marlin Mania was sweeping the state, and everyone was excitedly anticipating opening day in Miami.

At this time in my career, I was owner of a well-established lock shop in downtown Fort Lauderdale. In one of the business towers that I serviced the master key system and locks, the Marlins set up their first corporate office. Wayne Huizenga hired and placed Mr. Dave Dombrowski as General Manager at this time to build and guide Florida's newest sports franchise.

Now one day I was driving in my service van by the tower in downtown Fort Lauderdale, where the Marlins worked at their corporate office on the seventh floor. I spied a fat brown wallet lying in the hot sun on a busy street. I slammed on the brakes and jumped from my service van to quickly retrieve the fat brown leather wallet. How someone could lose such a beautiful wallet was beyond me. Before I could explore who, this belonged to, I decided to return to my shop only a few blocks away. When I returned to my shop I looked inside to see if I could identify the owner and return the wallet to him. Opening the wallet, I was shocked to see a minimum of forty credit cards. There was not a single dollar in the leather but dozens and dozens of credit cards. All with the name of Dave Dombrowski. How could one man accumulate so many cards, I thought! I saw a business card that identified him as the general manager of the newly formed ball club "The Florida Marlins." Wow! I thought, As I dialed the number I had for the Marlins, he is lucky I found this and not one of the many transients that filled the streets of Fort Lauderdale. I bet you could buy lots of Mogan David wine on these cards. The phone rang and then was answered by a Marlin Receptionist. Asking for Mister Dombrowski, he soon came on the line. I explained that I had found his wallet in the street and wanted to reunite him with it. He was overjoyed with emotion and explained to me that he was on his way to ship a package and had placed the wallet on top of his car, his mind being elsewhere, he had unlocked the doors and climbed in, forgetting the wallet sitting on top of his vehicle. "My God," he exclaimed, "I have so many credit cards I had no way of knowing where to start or how to put holds on them." Yes, you got a bunch of them." I replied. "Listen, Mister Dombrowski, I am leaving my office, and I know you are on the seventh floor of one of the buildings that I service. Give me thirty minutes and I will bring your wallet right over." "Thank you, Thank you. I am remarkably busy today and I would appreciate that."

Thirty minutes later I am standing in front of the receptionist desk in the Marlins seventh floor Lobby. Having explained to the receptionist the situation she ushers me into the General Manager's office. From behind a pile of papers I see Mister Dombrowski's head, and he waves me over while talking on the phone. He stretches out his hand and with a little motion of his fingers he indicates he would like his wallet. Placing the wallet in his outstretched hand, he quickly slips it into his coat and turning his back to me continues with the phone conversation. I realize he is not going to acknowledge my presense he might slip me a twenty or a few bucks for finding his wallet but no, not even thank you. That is OK I say to myself, I did a good deed and recognition for that is not important. People are strange and I got work to do, so I departed his office with a goodbye wave to the back of his head.

I guess the story could end here but it does not.

Three days later I received a box delivered by UPS from the Marlins. Looking inside is a black ballcap with a big teal colored "F." A small note that says "Thanks, Dombrowski" Awesome! I brag to my staff about the virtues of charitable deeds and realized that was Dave's way of thanking me.

The next day a second package arrives and when I look inside, I find these cute Marlin pins of a swordfish in marlin attire swinging a bat. A possible Promo in the future and a gift to me. Wow! I am impressed. For the next few weeks, the boxes started rolling in and I had cool stuff like a mini teal baseball bat, Bobble-head dolls, and just cool stuff. Staff became excited to see what I would receive next, thank you, Dave.

Opening day for the Marlins was drawing close and, in a few weeks, the first game of the season would be the first game for the Marlin Franchise. I could see it now, a package arriving and inside two tickets for opening day. My mind wandered and I dreamed of tickets with access behind the home plate and a splendid view of the field. Peanuts, hot dogs, and cold beer, Baseball is great fun. I was getting excited and any day now that package would arrive. Then life happened.

Arriving home from work one afternoon I did my usual and sat down in the recliner, with a cold adult beverage, to watch the national news broadcast. Getting comfortable, I glared at the television as I saw breaking news scrolling across the bottom of the broadcast. They interrupted the news with; "Just in with Breaking News, Dave Dombrowski, General Manager of the Florida Marlins Franchise, while attending a meeting of all baseball GM's, has just died of a massive heart attack." The anchor went on with the details, but that one main line was enough for me.

Of course, I felt sad for Dave and his family, my heart goes out to them, Dombrowski was a great American.

Me, I never received a package after that day. No more little gifts and no Opening Day tickets to the greatest game on earth.

In the immortal words of the great Paul Harvey; the one line he would say at the end of all his radio broadcast, "And that my friends, is the rest of the story."

# Chapter 17

# Not a Locksmith Story

Not a locksmith story

Back in the early seventies I took a four-year break from locksmithing to sail the seas and visit foreign ports of call. As a locksmith the pressure can grow inside from making difficult judgement calls in desperate situations. Your psyche gets overwhelmed and the time comes when you have got to take a step back. I am sure there are other professions with similar pressures; and a change of scenery is important to avoid cracking or even insanity. In the seventies I chose the Navy, In the Eighties I switched careers and wound up in the restaurant business.

Restaurant business I did not know it was insanity at all levels and varying degrees. But a change was needed, and I made it so.

I started out waiting tables at TGIF, you know, Thank God it's Friday. The different foods and assorted drinks, bottles of wine, a great introduction to the industry. The customers, the people, happy, always celebrating something. Spending money, drinking alcohol and leaving big tips. Big tips if you did not screw up. Fellow staff members, Men and women, all new to this line of work, having fun and laughter. After the clients departed the partying would hit a new level of excitement.

The hard part was not to spend all the money you had worked all night making. Many a waitress or waiter would wake up the next day with a killer hangover and no money to pay the rent or buy a Starbucks coffee.

Trading in my red and white striped shirt, funny hat, and suspenders, I went to work for a small respectable restaurant called Kaleidoscope in Coconut Grove, Florida. The dress attire was casual and the food a high caliber. From the second floor the dining room overlooked 'the Coconut Grove Playhouse' and the Kaleidoscope was a fun spot to grab a bite to eat before performances.

Matinees were extremely busy times, women trying to squeeze in lunch with friends, and we would be inundated with a sea of 'Blue Hair.' Blue Hair as in elderly women dressed to the 'Nines' with white hair piled high in tinted hair dos on top of their heads. Before one Matinee I had taken on a table of twelve ladies and was pressed to keep pace with their incessant demands.

Coffees and iced teas had flowed from the kitchen, soups and salads had been served and cleared. Twelve entrees had been placed politely in front of twelve demanding women. I retired to the 'back of the house' to catch my breath and sanity.

Piercing the noise of the kitchen and the frontal lobe of my brain, I heard the desperate pleas of a high pitched voice, "Waiter! Waiter!" coming from one of my twelve ladies. Thinking she had cut one of fingers off from the urgency in her voice, I rushed to the table to find a frazzled overweight red-faced patron pointing at her plate.

"Mam, may I ask, what is wrong?"

Without looking up, she yells, "Waiter, Waiter! I've got a bad potato!"

The plate held several small white peeled potatoes cooked firm to the bite. I asked, "Which potato, Mam?" And without hesitation she pointed to a slender white potato she had nudged off to the side. "That one!"

I picked up her dining room fork and stabbed the offending potato, holding it aloft for the whole table to see. I said, "Bad potato! Baaad potato! You have been a very bad potato." Returning the potato to her plate and the fork back beside her plate, I finished with, "if that potato gives you anymore trouble, you just let me know."

The table was silent, her mouth hung open, eyes wide, she was not sure what had happened. The restaurant patrons seated at other tables applauded as I walked away, and the table as a group left a very generous tip.

Kaleidoscope had a sister restaurant in Coral Gables and at times they would enlist the waitstaff to help with service on extremely busy nights. I was fortunate to be recruited one evening and got assigned to a group of tables in the loft. Five tables up a steep wooden staircase. The night had gone smoothly, I was young and the trudging of food up and down the stairs was a minor annoyance.

Late in the evening a table of five young adults decided to end their meal with a liquor aperitif. The choice was Flaming Sambucas. Now Flaming Sambucas are served up, in a martini glass with three coffee beans floated on top and flaming as in 'on fire.' The flame on these sambucas was a beautiful shade of blue with green highlights and it made a very impressive drink to serve and for clients to end the evening.

I held the tray at the service bar with the martini glasses filled to the rim, the bartender quickly lit the drinks, and I proceeded to make my way across the crowded restaurant to the staircase that led upstairs.

As I crossed the room, I noticed a tiny trail of liquor run down one of the glasses and a small blue green flame chased it down the stemware. When I reached the stairs, I began to climb the steps slowly balancing the overfilled drinks as best as I could.

Yes, the Sambuca was sloshing out and all five martini glasses now had flames running down to the tray. I was nervous and hurried which only made it worse, because halfway up the tray filling with spillage was ablaze in blue green fire.

I was starting to panic as the flames, not content to remain on the tray, moved to my bare arm in a dazzling display of pyrotechnics. Customers were watching open mouthed, as threw the tray against the wall next to the staircase and the blue flames licked the wallpaper, charred it, and the flames burned out. The owner from the front podium was watching and suddenly started yelling in German.

I was never invited back to work there, I do know why.

In my quest for perfection, I did work in a French restaurant in Fort Lauderdale, 'Pettibon's.' The owner/chef was amazing, and my knowledge of food spiraled to new heights. Gueridons, thin carts with wheels, were used at times for table side service. From Ceaser salad to carving Rack of Lamb, the gueridon was an invaluable tool for tableside service.

One night a young couple had come for dinner and had ordered the whole grilled seabass. A delicious dish with a mild white flaky flesh. The fish was served whole, filleted, and deboned tableside. Plated and served with the trimmings. My problem was that as I dissected the fish with two spoons, inside was a second fish. Obviously, it had been swallowed before the bigger fish had been caught. The young lady started to gag, and her husband was blinking rapidly. To ease the tension all I could think of saying was, "Sorry, looks like we got to charge you for two fish now!" And when I asked, "Mam, would you like the big fish or the smaller one?" that is when they left.

Worked a grand opening for a friend in New York City at a new place called 'Cava Canine' House of the dog. The chef did authentic Roman cuisine, unheard of back in that time. He served a fish paste at the table that was fermented in clay pots, which marinated on his rooftop patio in the East Side of New York. On opening day, he had rabbits, and small people in costumes, running amuck in the dining room. What a wild night that was.

Working in a beautiful hotel on the beach of Fort Lauderdale, we had a table one afternoon of three nationally renowned preachers and their wives, seated round a table overlooking the Atlantic Ocean. They were dressed in extremely expensive clothing; the men's suits had to go for over a thousand dollars each and the women all flashed large diamonds and gold to outdo each other. They were happy and laughing, in good spirits, after all it was Sunday and for them Pay-day. As I poured the Cristal Champagne keeping the glasses full, the conversation centered around how to get the most out of the pockets of their parishioners. What tales they told of fleecing little old ladies on the flat plains of the panhandles, separating the people from their crumpled dollars to the last nickel. But even the rich would get a bulls-eye tattooed to them. No one would be spared their line of hypocrisy, as I listen to the flow of thievery. They would toast, Champagne is expensive and God is good."

Ended up down in the Virgin Islands, late eighties, opening and working a small, tiny restaurant called 'Café St. John' with a partner. Not being a chef per say, I did find myself working in the kitchen prepping, line cooking, and washing dishes. The menu leaned heavily on 'Continental Cuisine. Things like, Veal Oscar, Stroganoff, Entre-cotes, and one of my favorite dishes, Bouillabaisse. Bouillabaisse is a Mediterranean dish of several fresh seafoods cooked delicately over an open flame with white wine, spices and saffron. The dish takes time, and my menu reflected that in small print. 'Please allow forty-five minutes cook time on this dish." It was always worth the wait; besides, you were on a small island there was no place to rush off to.

The last ferry from the mainland, on a rainy night, deposited two couples fresh from New York onto the wharf. It being almost ten they hustled inside my establishment, famished, tired and hungry. Of course, the two men ordered the Bouillabaisse, and, in the kitchen, I begun the process of assembling the ingredients. Thirty minutes later the two couples, tired from traveling and adult libations, began to grumble the food was taking too long. At the forty-five-minute mark the couple gets up and walk towards the door. I stop them at the doorway and explain that the food is ready and perhaps they would like to return to the table. "Oh no." They are leaving and not paying for a thing. "I can box it to go for you; it will only take a minute." I explain. But no, no, no. is their response.

So, in a nice voice I explain, "you knew the food was going to take forty-five minutes to prepare. The waitress told you that, and I am sure you saw this on the menu. Now I put a lot of expense and time into these dinners. You do not need to eat them, but you damn well are going to pay for them!"

They did use some colorful language and then defiantly yelled, "we'll call the police on you!" I could not help but start laughing. Finally, I gain control and to the two men I say, "let me help you with that". They have a puzzled look on their faces as I  ask one of the waitresses to send out the dishwasher, and in noticeably brief time a stocky Island man in apron steps through the doorway into the dining room.

"Gentlemen, allow me to introduce you to the Chief of Police on this island. You see guys, this island is small and we all moonlight at times for extra money." The Chief removes his apron and folding it neatly, places it on a chair, squaring his shoulders he looks at the two New York men and ask, "Now what is the problem?"

The men both say, "No Problem." Paid their tab and hustle out the door to enjoy the rest of their vacation.

Later that night the Chief of Police and I sat down at a table and enjoy a delightful seafood dinner of Bouillabaisse with just the right amount of saffron.

Restaurants are filled with wonders and stories, the allure of fast money, and once you are in this business it is hard to get out. I found myself suddenly spending six or seven years in the trade, and no better off than the day I started. Looking around I found it was time to fall back, and so I returned to my old profession Locksmith.

# Chapter 18

# Boats, the first call

Boats, the First Call

Getting my first boat call as a locksmith was exciting and I leaned back in my chair, closed my eyes, and just let my imagination run wild. I could see the headlines in the papers, "Locksmith who specializes in marine hardware retires rich and happy at an early age." All of this, after only one boat call, my dreams are falling into place.

On the phone the captain of the boat had explained to me that his one-hundred-and-twenty-foot yacht was in need of lots of lock work. Possible all new hardware. When he asked, "do you work on boat hardware?" I almost screamed into the phone, "you betcha, I'll be right over."

Boats, Yachts, Captain, and crew, owners of yachts had money just falling out of their pockets, and I am going to get rich on this job! Well not rich, but this was not some little old lady I was trying to separate from her social security money. On this job my motto will be, "Have no mercy!" This was the job I had been waiting for my whole life. On a yacht in the sun, salt water and clean work for a captain who assures me money is no problem. "I am Locksmith, hear me roar!"

Okay, after an exciting drive to the marina, I parked and loaded up my toolbox, added a drill motor, and threw an extension cord over my shoulder. I made sure I got two hammers: one large and one even larger. An assortment of wrenches, screwdrivers, all in metric and standard sizes. I stuff lock picks, screwdrivers, ink pens, and pencils in my pockets. I scratched my head and thought, what am I forgetting, oh yes, my bill book for invoicing, and an extra battery for my Makita drill. Gee, I am ready, let's go!

Trudging through the parking lot, after parking at the far end, I noticed the endless rows of cars, so many rows of cars. Walking in the hot sun I entered the boat yard and headed to the Dock Master's office. Finding the Dock Master, I give him the name of the yacht and ask where she lies. "Dock Q, and young man," he says to me, "the sun is brutally Hot today. You should be wearing a hat." "I will be fine, just point the direction of 'Q' dock." "Ok, young man," and he continues in that slow southern drawl, "You see that sea wall way down there? Turn right and at the very end of the seawall is a pier. Walk down to the end of that pier and you will find a long floating dock. That is Dock 'Q,' walk to the end of dock 'Q' and you will find your boat. Wow, I think as I start walking in the hot sun, maybe I should not have brought so many tools. As I near dock 'Q' I see the yacht for which I am searching. She is a real beauty, all fiberglass, aluminum, and money. The toolbox I am carrying has become so heavy that by the time I reach the gang plank I am wishing I had worn a hat. My head is cooked and my face red, the throbbing in my arm is unbearable from the weight of the toolbox. I am sure the pain will pass in a day or two, right now I am ready to make some money.

"Hey Captain," I yell out, "permission to come aboard? What do you mean I got to take my shoes off first? Okay, okay." I squat down to remove my shoes and notice I have a hole in my sock and my big toe wants to hang out. Not a particularly good first impression, but with all the money I am going to make, I plan to buy a new pair of socks. Now let's go to work.

The captain informs me that he is anxious for me to get to work but first I must leave that dirty old toolbox on the pier, next to my shoes. "No problem" I respond cheerfully. Then he adds, "please be careful with all those tools hanging out of your pockets. The white gelcoat on the bulkhead chips easily. And will be expensive to you to repair." Ouch, Ray, be careful, I say to myself.

He showed me the salon wing doors first, all teak and etched glass. Expensive I bet, and the captain whispers back, three thousand each door. The doors have mortised hardware, polished brass from the Federal Republic of Germany. The key cylinders have letters GSV stamped into the face. Never seen this stuff before, but what the heck, I am a locksmith, and I can fix anything.

The screws will not come out of the door to remove the locks; I am starting to sweat profusely in this eternally hot sun. I pull out my large hammer and channel lock pliers; all the screws need are a few good whacks and some brute force. Yet the screws will not break free. I go to my toolbox and grab the extra-large hammer, and I am sure this will work. No lock has ever defeated me. I detect a note of whining in the captain's voice as he sees the big hammer and implores me to please be careful. I sooth his fears and assure him I have never been beaten by a screw. He turns and hurries away muttering something like "I cannot watch."

Still the screws are stubborn, and I realize I need my big yellow Dewalt drill motor with variable speed and reverse. I grab a handful of drill bits tough enough to open a TL30 Mosler Safe. Returning to the door, I stand red-faced and breathing heavy, my hair is sticking up and my shirt tails hanging out. I catch the captain peeking around the corner of the long hallway. He does not look so good, and I wonder what is wrong with him.

Okay, I say to myself, this will not be easy money, but those screws are coming out. Hours later and soaking wet, I left the yacht with lock in hand and dragged my rusty old toolbox by the extension cord behind me. The sun is still beating down; I resist the urge to push my toolbox over the edge of the pier into the water.

I have promised the captain quick results. So, I called my friend, Kris. She is the world's Guru of boat hardware. I explain what I have and what I need, after emailing photos to her. She starts to laugh uncontrollably. Finally, she calms down and explains that this lock has not been manufactured for over ten years. That no repair parts are available on the face of the earth, I will need to have them made. I wish she would stop laughing, but that is ok, I honestly believe that no lock will ever defeat me.

I go to my local machine shop and have the needed parts fabricated and expedited. "How Much!" I cried out seeing the invoice, "that's very expensive." Yes, it is for a boat and money, the captain says it is not an issue. Now I have a working lock and prepare to return the next day to finish the project and make lots of money. I returned to the boat the following day, leaving most of my tools in the van. Installing the lock is smooth and easy. I anticipate writing the invoice when the captain turns to me and snaps, "are those ferrous metal screws you used to install my lock? Because if they are ferrous metal screws, they will be unacceptable!" "Yes," I whisper, "ferrous metal they are."

Once again, I face that long walk down the dock, I will need to find a hardware store that sells brass screws, return and complete the job. I yelled at the captain that I would return in the morning. "That's fine" yells back the captain, "just don't be later then nine, boat's going to sea." 'Ya! Ya!" I say as I blink in the glaring sun with a weak smile and hint of a migraine.

The next morning, I open my shop doors at eight and give some instructions to my staff. As I prepare to leave an emergency call comes in with a little old lady locked out of her apartment in a bathrobe. I gave her a quote and headed her way convinced that I would make the boat on time. Her lock opens easily, and I get her inside the apartment in record time. Giving her the invoice for 49.95 she starts the search for money to pay. I groan because I see her shaking a Piggy bank upside down and she is no longer in a hurry to complete the transaction. Finally, in nickels, dimes, and quarters she counts out 49.95.

It is after ten that I run to the seawall, make a right, and go down to the pier. Jogging down the wooden planks I jingle and jiggle with pockets filled with small coins. Standing on the floating dock 'Q' I see the miserable Dock Master, But no yacht, no captain.

I run up to the Dock Master waving my invoice in my hand, "Where is she?" I cry out. The startled Dock Master turns and then begins to laugh "Why, she's gone to Europe for the summer!" He howls with laughter and tears running down his cheeks.

# Chapter 19

# Boats and the Wealthy

B oats and the Wealthy

I love boats, all kind of boats, power boats, sail boats, even submarines. I have always lived near, or on the water, and boats have played a crucial part in my life. House boats are ok, sailboats are cooler, and mega yachts are the best. I have never lived on a mega yacht, but I have worked on hundreds of them in Fort Lauderdale, Florida and the beauty, the power, and the money these boats reflect is impressive.

Thanks to the company I worked for, I started making lots of boat service calls. I was fortunate to work on a couple of the Denison "series" mega yachts named after Ian Flemming novels. MY 'Thunderball' and MY 'Octopussy' are vivid in my memory from the James Bond collection. Both equipped with Kawaneer water jets on the underside there were no props or screws, and the boats were very fast. Fast for boats over one-hundred twenty feet in length and soaked in luxury and Jamaican Rum. The motor yacht 'Octopussy' would later end up grounded trying to cross a shallow sandbar in the Intercoastal of Fort Lauderdale, Florida. Sucking up old tires that anchored the sandbar, into the Kawaneer jets disabling  and almost sinking one of the most beautiful boats ever built.

One night I got a call to work on a green hulled boat with a red stripe around its perimeter. The boat, named 'Red Stripe' was a flagged Jamaican yacht named after the country's infamous beer, Red Stripe. Going into the salon of the vessel I noticed the long thick Shag carpet green in color, and the air heavy with the smoke and odor of marijuana. I had no doubts about which island of the Caribbean this boat hailed from as I watched the crew celebrating a successful day in the yards. Boats always provided wonderful color and stories, always amazed with the adventures and history.

I received a call many years ago from a boat broker that wanted to list this one hundred forty-foot yacht that had been sitting in a paint shed at a local marina for many years. To sell the boat it had to undergo a survey first. The surveyors had seen a locked safe in the owner's stateroom. No combination could be found, and the boat could not be listed and sold until the safe was opened. Hence the broker had called me to expedite the situation.

I dispatched myself to the job and met up with the captain who appeared to be old. Wait, back up, he was incredibly old. Chatting with the captain he explained that this boat had been sitting in this paint shed for eight years at a cost of three hundred dollars a day. The captain's job was to come on the boat every morning to run the bilge pumps, make sure she was floating, and then go home. For this he said his annual salary was eighty thousand dollars a year. Wow! What a wonderful job. When the boat was sold, he was going to retire, he explained, his work being done.

The boat had been owned by a lady in Texas who had died. The trust fund was selling off all assets to be divided by the heirs. The captain explained that the safe was empty and he was going home, it was ten: thirty and he was tired. He pointed to the owner's stateroom, and He told me to open it, repair it, and send him an invoice, goodbye. I walked out to the parking lot, grabbing my tool bag, a battery powered drill, and some cobalt drill bits from my service vehicle. I walked back to the boat. Taking off my shoes [an unwritten law when working on yachts] before going inside, I entered the main salon then pushed onward to the owner's stateroom. Finding the safe in the corner of the room I analyzed the safe then coordinated my drill points to open the door. It was not a complicated opening, after thirty minutes I was ready to turn the handle and pull the door open.

The captain was right, the safe was empty, just dust. Packing up my tools to leave I turned to look one more time inside the safe and I noticed a small door set back with a keyhole at the top corner of the safe. Might as well do a complete job I thought, and picking the little lock on the small door, it opened right up. I gasped as I looked inside, the compartment was stuffed with large denomination bills. Taking a step to pause, my mind raced. I needed to find that Captain before he went to bed. Finally, I turned and ran up the stairs to the gangplank, I made my way across and through the Marina to the marina office. Asking politely about a number for the captain, the young man seated at the desk was happy to give it to me. I called the captain and explained about the safe, the small door and all the cash inside. He needed to return to count this money and verify the amount with me before I could leave.

"Can't you just count it?" he whined. "No, I will not touch it until you join me in the stateroom. I do not want any questions aimed at my integrity later." He arrived in about twenty minutes, either he lived nearby, or he drove like Steve Mc Queen to get back to the yacht. We walked on the boat together and made our way down to the stateroom. I swung open the safe door and then opened the little tin door inside the safe. I swear his eyes teared up when he saw the contents. Removing the money from the safe we laid it out on the bed, most of it was hundred-dollar bills with a scattering of fifties and twenties. Together we both counted the money, and the total was over sixty-six thousand American dollars. I presented him with my invoice for three-hundred, work rendered, and he replied just to send it to the corporate office.

Leaving the yacht, I noticed the captain was in good spirits and smiling. He turned to me and said, "You know what? I am going to have a nice retirement. Thank you, Ray." We left the boat and parted ways. I always wondered if that money ever made it back to the dead woman's trust fund.

I thought this was an interesting tale, and when I got home that night, I could not wait to share this with my wife. When I got to the part where we counted the cash and then went our separate ways, my wife punched me in the head, knocking me out of my chair. "What the Hell," I cried out. She stood over me with her hands on her hips and fire in her eyes, "You are telling me you found sixty-six thousand dollars on an old yacht with no one on board. Money that no one knew about, just sitting there for eight years. Money that was put there by an old lady that is now dead! We are eating Hamburger every night, and you called this old retiring captain to come and get it?"

"I am not feeding you tonight, I am going to bed."

# Chapter 20

# Boats, Boats and more Boats

Boats, Boats, and more Boats

I received a phone call one autumn day from my boat hardware supplier, Shea Patrick. After some small talk, she informed me that she had received a request to do some lock work for a Sheik from Saudi Arbia. She informed me that this Sheik had a large mega yacht, over two hundred feet in length, called "The Golden Odessey." And this sheik had made an unusual request.

This word unusual, caught my attention, I loved jobs that started out that way because that meant something in the work was going to be far from the norm, and that meant it was going to be exciting and financially beneficial.

I asked my friend for the details, and she began by saying that I would need to travel to Jacksonville from Fort Lauderdale, to survey the doors and hardware involved in the project. She asked my rate, and I pushed back with two thousand dollars a day. With no hesitation or counteroffer, she agreed.

Driving to the boat I got there in the early morning. The boat was big with a Filipino crew and at their insistence I removed my shoes, putting on blue paper-thin booties over my socks. I requested permission to come aboard and meet the captain; the captain was pleasant and helpful. After explaining what I was going to do he explained the basic lay out of the yacht and a reminder that lunch would be served at twelve in the crew quarters and hoped to see me at that time. "Please go ahead and do your survey and move about the yacht freely, as he waved me off.

When doing a hardware survey, I list every door separately noting the swing, the lock manufacturer, the lock function, and color. What grade of hardware, hinges, door closers, and photos. 'The Golden Odessey' had multiple decks and multiple doors, or hatches, on each deck. Starting at the main deck I moved past the jacuzzi to the main saloon dripping in elegance I noted all doors and moved into the dining room. The dining room was divided from the salon with a large saltwater aquarium that took up the entire wall. The aquarium filled with so many fish I was dazzled.

Standing in front of the glass with a long-handled net stood a young man. He informed me he was working on the aquarium. After a short and pleasant introduction, he informed me he was from the London Ocean Aquarium in England, one of the largest in the world. 'Wow so far and I thought I had traveled a long way." This was his part time ''gig' keeping this tank vibrant, it was beautiful, a collage of color and movement.

The dining room table was of substantial length and covered with Waterford crystal and several types of stemware. A Steward stood polishing the glasses one at a time.

Moving forward I found a hallway with various suites and at the end a large double door that opened onto the master suite, the Shiek's stateroom. Oversized and elegant, it had two spacious bathrooms. Noting all doors I moved onward and upward and found a movie room that led out aft to a large deck. Going forward I found rooms that I, could only guess at what their purpose was. I did discover a barbershop and beauty salon, a spa room and even a ship's store.

Finding some stairs I went up and found a second salon that led to a hallway with radio room, chart room and the bridge. One more door was hiding a stairwell that led to the helo deck, of course.

Returning to the main level I proceeded down a staircase and found a small hospital, empty, and doors that led aft to engine rooms and berthing for ship engineers. A workshop behind one door, a large laundry room, evaporators to make fresh water. It was all there. Going down one more level I entered the crew's quarters, a small dining room and a table piled high with various food.

I had timed it well, it was lunchtime. Sitting with the Captain, he told me some of the history of "The Golden Odessey" the ship was the only civilian ship to have been built in an American naval shipyard, and that it had been a gift from the American people to this important Shiek.

"The Golden Odessey" had a sister ship over three hundred feet in length called, "The Golden Shadow." It followed this yacht around the world, and it held all the toys for the Shiek and his friends to play with. The main deck held twin 30-foot Chris craft boats port and starboard. Various jet skis, and a pontoon plane on the aft deck, which could slide back onto the water and be airborne in minutes.

I returned home that evening after a tiring drive and typed up my report and survey. Forwarding everything to my friend, via fax. A couple of weeks later she called all excited and said, "we got the job." "What job is that?" I asked. "Why the Golden Odessey" she replied. "You are going to the BAE shipyard in Mobile, Alabama next week."

"And what will I be doing? I asked, you already have my report." To my question she replied, "Why the Shiek, wants all his hardware, all the locks, levers, and knobs, all the key cylinders, hinges and door stays, dipped in gold. After all Ray, you will be working on, 'the Golden Odessey." Laughing she added, "And our job is going to be to make her truly Golden."

At two thousand dollars a day I was happy to oblige. My only question was, "How soon can we start?"

A week later I cleared the background checks for BAE shipyards in Mobile, Alabama. After a tedious drive to the shipyard, I found myself standing in front of the ship, Golden Odessey. It was sitting out of the water on a concrete apron held tall with large wooden blocks. A long, tall ladder was the only way up, and on or off the boat. Back on board the ship It took two days to remove all locks bag and tag. It was demanding work; I just kept reminding myself that I was getting paid and paid well.

It took over a week to have them plated in gold, and then back to the boat with the tedious task of reinstalling all the hardware. Two more long days working in socks, my feet were killing me. Finally, it was done and 'The Golden Odessey' was now, truly golden.

# Chapter 21

# White Space

White space

Always looking for new ways to generate revenue in the locksmith industry, an unusual opportunity became available to us in North Miami Beach. Approaching a high-end fashion mall with tremendous foot traffic, we had this novel concept to open a kiosk on the mall floor and try our luck at selling safes, and high security products in an untested market environment.

After much pleading with mall management an agreement was reached to open a small kiosk. Wanting to sell safes, we found a safe wholesaler in Miami that was gracious enough to provide floor samples at no charge for our display. These safes of assorted sizes had high gloss paint finishes of unusual colors. Installing custom interiors that held drawers and ring trays in crushed velvet were works of beauty that made the safes unique and one of a kind. Installing digital electronic locks that worked on kinetic energy, created by oscillating the dial, was the touch of high tech that pushed our product over the top. We had created the designer safe, and people loved them.

That first year, safe sales topped two million dollars, all from a ten foot by ten-foot open air space. Keeping up with customers' demands for products was increasingly difficult and we had outpaced all Miami suppliers. I found myself pulling products from as far away as New York and California to meet consumer demands.

Manning a Kiosk from ten in the morning to late in the evening, seven days a week proved daunting. Being positioned in the center of the floor, like a large rock in a stream, with waves of people wandering by ensured a steady supply of customers, endless questions, and a large battle to keep trained staff on the floor Monday to Sunday. Sales were made and stories created.

I had designed one of the interiors to hold rolls of quarters nickles and dimes in colorful coin wrappers, and one day it proved to much for one young man passing by to ignore. He reached into the tall vault and grabbed a handful of rolled Quarters. Jumping a small safe he took off at breakneck speed. The young lady working with me witnessed this grievous behavior and yelled at me, "thief! Thief!" She took off running in pursuit of this young man. I joined the pursuit but being older found it difficult to keep up. I did manage to keep them in my field of vision as I trotted behind in pursuit, breathing heavily. A police officer witnessing this parade joined in the chase and we as a group careened down the crowded mall. People were being pushed aside and at one point everyone sprinted through an indoor fountain with shallow pond.

The chase deviated from the crowded mall, to jogging down long service corridors. Coming out a door we emerged one at a time into the sunlight at the first level of the parking garage, the young employee tackled the hapless young man bringing the pursuit to an end. Chugging up at the tail end, just in time to see the officer roll the perpetrator over and handcuff him, I breathlessly asked, "What happen?"

"He stole all the rolled quarters out of the safe, and I caught him!" She said with immense pride in her voice and not even breathing heavily. "Oh my God" I said as I bent down and pried one of the rolls of quarters from the young man's hand. "These are for display! and why would you steal them."

The police officer observed and commented, He has seven or eight rolls. Each roll is ten dollars! He almost made a good score." The thief looked down at his sneakers embarrassed to be caught.

"Look" I told the group. "These rolled quarters are for display. I made them myself." Quietly I peeled the paper wrapper off the roll. That revealed a large diameter wooden dowl, I had cut to size, shoved in a bank wrapper to reassemble a roll of Quarters. "I made these in dime and nickel wrappers also. I am not foolish enough to put real money out on the floor."

The officer at first angry then just started laughing, standing with his pants and shoes soaked said, "Why don't we just let him go?" "Yes" I agreed, "this wouldn't go far in court anyway." and the officer uncuffed him. I helped him to his feet. He was apologetic then off and running like a wet puppy, to escape before we could change our minds.

Standing at the Kiosk, it was a slow Wednesday morning, when the phone rang. Answering the woman on the other end of the line, she claimed, was the Concierge for Michael Jackson. "Oh Yeah?" was my response. "What can I do for The King of Pop?"

The Concierge went on, "Last night Mr. Jackson was a private shopper in the mall. This is when we arrange for a select few stores to stay open after Midnight, to accommodate our shopping needs without Mr. Jackson being overwhelmed by the fans."

"Sounds cool. But how can I help?"

"While we were walking through the mall, Mr. Jackson came across your Kiosk. He was quite impressed with your safes and would like to order two for his home in California." She explained. "He would like the Cherry Red, fireproof safe in the tall version, and a matching pearl white to stand next to it. Can you make the sale and arrange for delivery?"

"Yes of course," was my answer. "Will you be paying with check or with credit card?" She had a credit card and suddenly I knew she was legit. That is how I sold two safes to Micheal Jackson. The best news was that the safes were built in California, and shipping was inexpensive and quick.

A day later the mall security called me down to their office. "Ray," the security officer stated, "You got to see this." There on his oversized monitor he brought up my Kiosk on the screen. I could tell it was late at night, the mall was deserted, and the lighting had been dimmed.

"Wait for it." He said to me, and after a few minutes a group of people came into view. Of course, I recognized the 'King of Pop' right away, and he almost walked past the safes. But then he stopped and on the hard marble floor he "Moon Walked" around the display. Very impressive.

Many celebrities shopped in the mall. Many I did not recognize because they often wore disguises, and many I just did not know. A constant flow of sports athletes stopped to talk security and buy safes. One of my favorites was Alonso Morning, basketball great and center for the Miami Heat. The guy was down to earth, friendly, and funny, very human. Some were jerks but if they were buying, their cash was as green as the next guy's.

James Canne, stopped by one evening with his wife and spent about an hour talking and laughing over stories. Again, real people with no phony bologna. It was rare to come across someone that was obnoxious to the point, I did not like them.

I was selling safes to everyone, everywhere. I sold a couple hundred hotel safes to someone in Key West, and I took the time to personally deliver the product. I sold and shipped via DHL ten large safes to someone in Africa, and two days later sold ten thousand dollars in safes to a Mexican and dropped ship them to Mexico City.

It was going so well I opened a second store in West Palm Beach mall. This store looked like High Tech, and with all the extra floor space I expanded into cameras and advanced electronics, Access control, monitoring systems, and such. Again, it was met with success, and I began to slowly spiral into hell.

The problem was one of people's logistics. Running a shop in Broward County was tough, the business required constant attention overseeing security projects and staff. The Kiosk in Dade County and store front in Palm Beach County were a seven day a week operation, which ran past ten every night. Staff would suddenly not show up or call in sick. I would fill these voids driving long distances and would end up not getting home till Midnight.

Delivery and installations were growing, requiring more and bigger crews to honor customer commitments. Sure, I had a large bundle of cash stuffed in my mattress, and yet I was slowly going mad as the job started to age me and wear me down. Then something horrible happened that saved me. 911, the Twin Towers came down.

The master mind that flew the first plane into the first tower was from Palm Beach; his backyard was in close proximity to the mall. The world became filled with fear and malls suddenly were under attack by pranksters. People stopped shopping.

Evil people were throwing baby powder on floors in the department stores. It became a daily thing for the fire department to evacuate the mall and set up emergency showers to decontaminate or hose off the people, clients, and store employees. Everyone stopped shopping and coming to work. The once vibrate malls became empty cavernous halls. With no sales I could not continue to pay staff or the exorbitant lease to keep the doors open.

Closing the Palm beach store was a no brainer, and I figured since I was doing one, I might as well shut down the Dade County store also. What a huge mental relief it was to get back to running the single operation in Broward County.

I might mention that in closing the Palm Beach store, one of my delivery guys had loaded an expensive Stainless steel safe onto the platform on the back of his truck. He was bringing it down to the Broward store to place it on the store floor. He failed to secure the four foot seven hundred pound safe and did not close his tailgate.

Yes, on Interstate 95 the safe slid off into traffic. No one hit the safe, Thank God, but a film crew close by found it interesting enough to document the event and get it on the evening news. The driver was able to lift the safe back onto the truck using a little physics and lots of adrenaline. Of course, the safe had a horrible case of road rash. I had to let it go at a very substantial discount.

# Chapter 22

# Bits and Pieces

B its and Pieces

Life takes on a glow of its own when wearing the hat of a locksmith. You are no longer one of the masses but an individual endowered with unique skills to solve complex problems that many find daunting. A respect that comes from rising above mere mortality to a level of professionalism that escapes most men. Is it possible, electricians or plumbers feel the same elated feelings of grandeur as a locksmith, when resolving a complex issue?

When jobs are going smoothly the adulations roll in but when something goes awry, watch out. You stand alone. This reminds me of a safe deposit box I once drilled for an incredibly old man. As I drilled and worked the lock to achieve the 'opening' he kept poking me with his cane. A contemptuous old fart that kept saying things like, "hurry up." "What is wrong? Don't know what you're doing?" When he finally jabbed that cane in my ass, I turned to him, pulled the cane from his feeble hands, and broke it over my knee. That hurt, "Call someone else" I told him and left the bank. One of the rewards of working for yourself is you can tell bad actors to flick off.

I was repairing a lock on a vault door for armored car service. It was to be a new location, and the building was under extensive renovation. The lock in the banking world is referred to as the 'belly button lock,' a plunger or 'push in to lock' at about the height of your belly button. Its purpose is to lock the large handle in place to avoid the possibility of getting locked inside. Making two keys and screwing the new lock to the interior of the safe door my work was almost finished. When a young man, dragging a ladder and toolbelt with tools asked if I could help. "Sure, why not?" I responded.

He explained that he needed to adjust the alarm contact at the top of the vault door. He asked if I could push the door shut with bolts extended, but do not spin the dials, as that would lock him in. I had the combos and said not to worry, "I will stand guard at the vault door to ensure things go smoothly. By the way," I told him, "There is no electricity in the vault. No light, it will be pitch black." Cheerfully he held up his cellphone with its built-in flashlight. "No problem."

He stepped into the vault and pulled the door shut. I gently turned the large spoke wheel to engage the bolts with the frame, not touching any of the three dials. I could hear him whistling inside as he banged his ladder into place and made his adjustments by the light of his cellphone.

After five minutes he happily called out to say that he was finished, to please open the door. Sure, I responded and started to turn the chrome spoke wheel. It did not budge.

My heart skipped a few beats, and panic was entering the base of my core. I knew I did not touch the dials, so how can the handle not turn? From inside the safe I could hear the alarm guy say, "Quit fooling around, please, open the door."

"I'm trying, the wheel won't turn!" my voice an octave higher than it should be. "It's dark in here." was his response. My brain was racing with what could have gone wrong. I felt ill, and I had an urge to go get lunch. Let someone else discover the missing alarm tech. Then the realization came to me what might have gone wrong. "Did you by any chance push in the 'belly button lock'?" I asked. "No. No!" he replied at first. Then after a long pregnant pause he whispers, "my foot did hit something as I was climbing the ladder, let me check with my light. Wait, yes, there is a little lock, it seems to be pushed all the way in."

"Where are the keys? I gotta get out of here." His voice now shrill and filled with dread. "The keys" I tell him, "Are in my pocket and I have no way of giving them to you. But that is what has locked the 'spoked wheel' in place. Do you like thin crust pizza?" I ask. "Because that is the only thing that I will be able to slide under that vault door." "Not funny," he says. "Yes, you are right. Besides your air supply will run out long before the pizza gets here." Now he just whines.

I ask, "Do you have any lock picks?" "No," he replies, "I do have a battery powered drill with me and a small drill bit." "Well, thank the Lord, I am going to tell you exactly where to drill that lock and get you out. You only get one chance at this so use care and do not break the bit." After an informative discussion he carefully drills the lock and soon I am able to spin the wheel and retract the locking bolts. The music "Free Bird" is playing in the background.

In the 1960's I spent a lot of time traveling between Tampa and Miami. At the time, the only two routes were US Highway 27 that ran above Lake Okeechobee or the Tamiami trail that ran underneath the lake from Naples to Miami.

Taking the two-lane scenic route, through the Everglades you would visually be bombarded with road signs, and because the terrain was so boring you would read them all. My favorite was a group of signs fashioned from dried out Cypress trees. A tall skinny post with a cross-member branch. Across the top branch, the words, T-Bones

.25 cents ten miles. And below the name of the restaurant. Driving further the sign would repeat itself, T-Bones .25 cents, eight miles. Your mouth would water and belly growl as the signs continued mile after mile with the promise of .25cent T-Bones. Finally, the restaurant would appear on the horizon and as you closed in, with your eyes scanning the parking lot for an empty spot, you would see the final Cypress stick sign across from the restaurant,

T-BONES WITH MEAT 12.95.

Got a call one day to go to this boat and check out an old safe. Upon arrival I was taken to the owner's stateroom and showed a small safe mounted at eye level in the closet. I quoted three hundred dollars to open the safe assuming it was not going to be difficult. The captain explained that the boat and safe were eight years old. The safe was never opened, to his knowledge, and the combination was long gone.

I assumed I would need to drill a small hole to peek inside, but first I needed to make sure the wheels and parts were all operating correctly. Spinning the dial four or five times I stopped at fifty, and when I spun the dial back in the opposite direction, it came to a sudden stop at eighty-five. The safe was open and the captain almost fainted as he gripped the closet door for support. He claimed I was the best damn locksmith he ever saw. And that was the easiest three hundred dollars I ever made.

The captain did call me again from the Amalfi Coast in Italy. He had another safe, locked, and he wanted me to explain to this Italian locksmith how I opened safes. I had to let him go saying it was a touch, a gift. I could not teach that over the phone.

# Chapter 23

# The Law

T he Law

Sometimes law enforcement gives me the chuckles. For many years I have worked with different departments of law enforcement, from FBI to ICE to DEA. Even working with local police departments, they have had me laughing until I peed myself. Now I do not infer any disrespect to the men and women who have undertaken these serious and dangerous careers, yet there are times when you see their human side, and you've got to love them.

I had a police chief of a small town in South Florida call me to meet him at his office. He took me into a backroom and showed me, scattered on the floor, an estimate of fifty fireproof floor safes. The safes were of inferior quality and small in size. I will not reveal the brands. "What's this?" I asked while counting the lock boxes scattered on the floor. The chief said the safes had come out of apartments across town from 'small time' drug dealers. He needed to clear the room out and needed to know how much it would cost to open the lot. "I want to open them, inventory them, and throw the safe away. I need my room back!" Laughing I said, "Got to charge you one hundred dollars a safe, and you get to tell me when to stop." With a puzzled look He scratched his head, "I need them all open, but yeah, we got a deal, I will go grab some detectives to help inventory and you go grab your tools."

When I returned, I carried a five-foot crowbar hammer and large screwdriver. Looking the chief in the eyes, I kicked the closest safe to me over on its back. Jamming the crowbar into the crack between the door and body of the safe, pushing hard on the crowbar the door gave way and swung open with a large pop sound. "That is one hundred dollars!" I cried out. The chiefs eyes grew wide. "Let's move on," I yelled.

Kicking the second safe over I repeated the process and roared out "that is Two hundred dollars." Now I kicked the third safe over, and I quickly popped that open and turning to look the chief in his eyes I, and all the detectives in the room yelled out, "That is three hundred dollars!"

'Stop! Stop!" yelled the Chief. "I got you, and I only have one Question for you. How much you want for that crowbar?" Still laughing I replied, "why One hundred dollars." And the detectives in the room laughing all roared, "That is four hundred dollars!"

One day a young, uniformed police officer walked into my shop. Asking for me, he explained that he needed a set of 'Bump Keys.' "Bump keys," I repeated. "You want a set of those specialty keys that you can insert into a lock, rap the key on its head and unlock the door?" "Yes, I need them to perform my job. I am a police officer as you can clearly see." Then with a smirk he added, "you need to expedite this."

With a deep sigh, I agreed. "Sure" I said Let me get right on this." Turning I reach out for the phone and from behind me I could hear his high-pitched voice ask, "What are you doing?"

"Well," I said," "I am calling the Chief. Got to make sure you are authorized to have these tools. The Chief and I are good friends, and you are lucky, because I got his number right here. Now tell me what your name is?" and as I turned back to the counter, all I could see was his butt go out the glass door. In seconds I heard the tires squealing on the hot asphalt. Guess he was not coming back for those bump keys.

The FBI had a large office in Fort Lauderdale, and the guys were some of my best customers. They all had to own a set of lock picks, but not a small set. Always they would buy the sets that had flaps that unfolded with row upon row of picks and hooks and spiral key extractors. It was a dizzy array of equipment guaranteed to open any lock. Me, I carried a small slim leather case with only three tools. I would make my own picks because I liked the handles to be larger and more comfortable than what you could find store bought. My kit contained A rake pick, a hook pick, and a tension wrench or what some called a turning bar.

The FBI agents would look at me in despair when they asked to see what my picks looked like. 'Poor locksmith' they thought. Could not even afford the Deluxe kit of 192 factory stamped lockpicks. How embarrassing for me.

What the agents did not realize was that I was picking two dozen locks on average a day. The FBI agents hoped someday to pick one.

The call from the FBI came in and the problem was they had seven evidence rooms secured with high security locks and the doors were locked tight with no keys. All the agents had taken shots at trying to open these doors with no success. At the end of seven days, they did get one room opened, the first time I ever saw a chainsaw used to gain egress because desperation had set in. The men needed their evidence.

As I surveyed the job, I saw the one door with a large, ragged square cut out. The building manager had made them stop and call me.

Specialty doors were extremely expensive. They howled with laughter when I pulled my thin worn leather pick case out with only three measly tools. Each agent quickly pulled their lock pick collections out and with big smiles and laughter, offered to let me use some of those fancy store-bought tools. "No thank you, do not want to spoil myself. I just need a little room to work." With quiet smirks they looked to the lead agent who had to tell me that all his men had been to FBI Locksmith School. "Don't be disappointed" in a condescending voice, "my men are the best, and they all gave it a shot. No luck. Just remember we still got the chainsaw".

The locks were expensive, excellent quality locks, and this was no simple task. It took me close to three hours to open all six doors. I removed the locks to take to my shop around the corner, dismantled, rekeyed, and reassembled the door hardware. Returning and installing the locks, the agents were no longer pretentious.

The Secret Service opened a new office in Miami, and I got a job selling and installing hardware on three doors. The specs had been supplied by a security consultant and the projected cost for each door tipped the scale at ten thousand dollars. That might sound high to the average person, not to government agencies. Each door had a digital Kaba Mas combination deadbolt. To operate the lock, you would oscillate the dial to create kinetic dial in a code and retract the bolt. Below was a grade one Mortise lockset with Medeco high security cylinders. In the frame grade one Folger Adams Electric strike, controlled by a Hess Scrambler keypad mounted on the exterior wall. On a scrambler keypad the numbers would bounce around like crazy and end up in various locations every time you used it.

The three doors protected the Armory and a clandestine Operation room.

The installation was a fun project, and it was cool to see all the Secret Service stuff, like the presidential limo.

A few months later a morning came when I got a call from the agent that was my Liaison to the Secret Service. In a desperate voice and in frantic words, he explained he had lost the combination to the armory and the president was coming to town. "Yes?" I replied, and there was this long pregnant pause.

"All our bullets, our long guns, everything is locked inside. Is there any way you can get us in?" he sounded desperate. "I can try, remember those doors are built to keep people like me out." "Ok," he replied, "Just get over here quick! We do not have a lot of time!" Racing to the site I was ushered in. Walking around the black presidential limousine I stood in front of the Armory door and reached out to touch it. It was going to be tough, but Suddenly I had an idea. In my truck I still had the installation template for the Kaba Mas combination lock. On the template it showed the location of the screws used to hold the lock to the door. The light bulb was shining over my head, by taping the template in the exact position I could mark the door and drill, with a tiny one-eighth" bit, the screws. I was lucky because when the drill bit touched the screws, they spun counterclockwise and backed themselves out of the door and out of the lock onto the floor. Removing the dial, I was able to just push the lock into the armory, open the door and the secret service was back in bullets. The process took fifteen minutes, the agents were floored, and so much for a ten-thousand-dollar door.

I once installed a push button combination lock on the employee entrance door for a local police department. The chief asked me to keep the combination simple for the police officers using this entrance. "How about one-two-three?" and the chief said that would be fine.

Maybe a month went by before I got the call to come to replace the lock. When I arrived, I noticed the old lock had a large bullet hole in it. "What happen?" I gasped. I was told that one of the night officers could not remember the combination and in anger he shot it off the door. I hope to never get pulled over late at night by that guy.

# Chapter 24

# Two Guys

T wo guys

Two guys walked into my shop late one afternoon and said they needed help getting two floor safes, located inside a closet in a bedroom, opened. Not being sure if I could help, I made an appointment to go to their home and survey the situation on the following day. Arriving the next afternoon, I parked out on the street. I noticed the ranch style home was situated in an affluent neighborhood with a Range Rover parked in the driveway. I assumed pricing was not going to be an issue.

The young couple greeted me at the door and began to explain how they had purchased the house less than a year ago. I was told of all the remodeling, painting, and money that they poured into the house. At one point they mentioned how they had acid washed the interior walls, flooding the floor of the house in water and acid. This had soaked and ruined the carpet in the bedrooms and closets, and they quickly had to remove the foul-smelling, soaked carpet.

In this process the couple had discovered two 'round door' floor safes once hidden by the carpet, buried in the concrete of the closet. With no combination and an insatiable urge to know what treasure was inside, they had turned to me for help. The obvious question I needed to ask first, "Have you reached out to the previous owner for help? They could still know the numbers to open these floor safes and save you a bucket full of money."

"Yes," they replied, "we did reach out, you may want to sit down, and we will tell you what happened. It is a horrible story." I love a story, and at the moment had no pressing business to attend to. So, I found a seat and the young men launched into quite a tale.

The home's previous owners had been entrepreneurs, engaged in the restaurant business. A married couple, the husband worked in the business, and the wife did the books, working from home. The twin safes had been installed in the floor to hold cash from the restaurant sales.

At some point in their marriage a disconnect must have occurred, and the wife had taken a lover. The two must have been bold because the clandestine trysts ended up in the home on more than one occasion. It was only a matter of time before the lover discovered the existence of the two floor safes in the closet. The Lover, being an individual of low moral fiber, one night confronts the woman in bed, and with pistol in hand, demanded she open the floor vaults. I guess she was surprised by the turn of events, and with some excuse she reached over to her nightstand and retrieved a small caliber handgun. Firing blindly, she struck the lover several times, till the magazine was empty. He of course fired back shooting her in the back and spinal cord, paralyzing her from the waist down.

He died of his wounds quickly as street justice prevailed. She lived paralyzed from the waist down.

The husband, hearing the sordid details of his wife's affair that night, was devastated. He vowed he would never step foot in that house again and filed for divorce a few months later. The wife was paralyzed and would be bed bound for the rest of her life. Never to experience the joys of sexual pleasure, Karmic justice.

"Wow! What a story. But what about the combinations, did you ask?" I inquired. "Oh yes, we did." replied the couple. She told us, "If that son of a bitch, that shot and tormented me could not get the combinations, You two don't stand a chance in hell of getting them!" Now that is one tough woman, I thought.

"Guys your safes, lets give them a look."  I crouched down in the cramped closet and tried to spin the dial. They would not budge. I also discovered that the safe heads would not spin or rotate in the 'can.' Turning to the men I explained that the acid wash had run down into the safe head and can, and done some damage and corrosion.

I ran out to the truck and grabbed a can of 'PB Blaster,' a corrosion inhibitor. I soaked in the dials and moving parts. With much tapping and banging with a hammer I finally got a dial to spin. Of course, I could tell that the dial was not 'picking up the wheels' and realized that the safe did not stand a chance of being opened by any known safe opening methods. I explained that the damage from the acid wash had been so serve that the safe heads were just one corroded mass of metal.

The two men, hearing the unwelcome news, became worried and rightfully so. "What if someone breaks into our home and discovers the two floor safes in our bedroom. The intruder could put a gun to our head and demand that we open it. With no known combination we both could be killed."

"Yes," I replied, "this scenario has played out more than once in life. I can recommend two options. First, you can hire someone with a jack hammer to bust up the concrete around those safes to remove them from your closet. This will allow you to use a cutting wheel to cut the cans open at the bottom and remove what contents are inside. Just remember that these two safes have filled with acid wash and water.

Whatever is inside is corroded, if paper or money expect mush. Your second option is much simpler. Since the safes sit below floor level, you can float concrete over the top and pretend that they never existed. Out of sight and out of mind."

As they looked at each other, I already knew what they were thinking. How would they ever sleep at night not knowing what loot was buried in their closet? They would proceed with option "A." I wished them the best of luck, recommending a few muscle guys for the project.

# Chapter 25

# Business is Business

Business is Business

I started working in the locksmith arena at the age of sixteen. Over those years, this ongoing effort has included fieldwork, office work, and travel aboard. Managing three locations in South Florida, my work involves automobiles, boats, residential towers, government agencies, and home renovations. All with unique challenges and constant surprises. Flexibility might be the keyword for survival in this field.

Meeting my fellow and brother locksmiths has always been educational, entertaining, and richly rewarding. Ninety nine percent are the salt of the earth. That one percent, watch out. These guys have egos the size of the Hindenburg Zeppelin. They project a facade of arrogance, believing that they are the only one with specialized skills, that God, himself had bestowed on these individuals. These individuals, I have come to realize, under the bravado, are woefully undertrained individuals lacking in the foundation of lock work and knowledge to facilitate a successful endeavor. The shortcomings of these individuals become obvious after a while and their life paths are littered with failure.

Later in my career I was approached by someone who looked upon my success with envy and jealousy. He had to let me know that he was a better locksmith than me. In those exact words he said, with all the sad bitterness inside him, "you're not a locksmith!"

I replied to him, "Perhaps you are right. I have always considered myself a businessperson. I have looked at this career through the lens of profit and loss, not who is better than who. At this moment I seem to be doing well, how about you?" Mentally the word 'Loser' popped into my head as he trudged back to some beat up old Astro van, I kept that to myself, no reason to sink to his level. He huffed and puffed away to find someone else to hurl insults at.

Around this time Broward County put out a request to bid on a project of two hundred padlocks for Port Everglades. Requests like this are not unusual. Government Bids enter the marketplace constantly, and everyone and their mothers sharpen their pencils and compete for the project. Because the scope is large the bids can be competitive, arriving from all corners of the state. Low bid was always the winner making it tough for small businesses to outmaneuver large conglomerates that worked on thin margins. Quietly I listen to people in the trade, distributors, to Locksmiths working out of their homes, all entering bids. Prices had dropped to four dollars a padlock on this bid. The man mentioned earlier had bid below what his cost was, desperate to win and have that government agency as a 'feather in his cap.' He was determined to win at any cost. As I filled out my bid sheet, I decided to make a smart play, and I entered a bid of over one hundred dollars a padlock. Also, the four hundred keys needed to go with the padlocks, most bidders were tossing in gratis. I asked for ten dollars for each key.

The day of picking the winner of the bid was at hand and the three lowest bids were called in to present the product, bid and explain the quotes. I, too, was asked to participate. Standing in a hallway with my antagonist, he explained how he had lowballed the bid and was a sure winner, He howled with laughter when I told him what my bid was. I was last to present and walked into a conference room filled with County bigshots from the Port Director to Chief Purchasing agent. The Director of the Port looked up and laughing said, "I see your bid is one hundred and twelve dollars a padlock, and you want to charge us ten dollars a key! Our lowest bidder is three fifty a padlock and seventy-five cents a key." The whole room was snickering. The director continued, "We asked you here because we just got to hear what is going on in your head. Please take the floor." Standing and facing the Director of the Port, I asked, "Why? Why are you requesting two hundred padlocks? What is wrong?"

He got a little serious and responded that the locks were for all the gates and entry points to sensitive areas of the port. The problem was Officers of the Sheriff's Department and port facilities personnel were losing keys at an excessive rate, and keys were being made all across town. "To be honest we have no idea who has access to our port, after 911, we are terrified of a terrorist attack. Our solution is to keep buying and changing padlocks to try to stay one step ahead of a calamity.

Quietly I said, "I have the solution for your problem. The product I am offering is key control. Let us put a high-grade padlock with a Borum steel shackle and shackle guard on these gates. The shackle is virtually impossible to cut, and extreme high resistance to picking, Match that with keys that cannot be duplicated without written authorization by you the director. The lock can be master keyed and rekeyed. Each of these keys we issue will be serialized and stamped with codes and assigned to personnel. Detailed key records will be kept, and you will know if someone misplaces or loses the key and exactly which gates that key opens. The keys will have the port logo and phone number. Should someone turn in a key, you can track the offending person and take appropriate disciplinary action. County employees will no longer be able to get a 'spare' to hide their carelessness and irresponsibility. I will provide a software program for tracking keys and padlocks; you will have the most secure port on the east coast. Oh, and no more endless buying of padlocks and keys. We now have control!" The room was quiet now, no more snickering. The director stood up and shook my hand and said, "Thank you, thank you for that expose, you may leave."

A week later I received the Req for two hundred padlocks and two hundred keys. Keys that only I could create. There was a patent in place and there was no wiggle room for any locksmith to get around that. The port bid was mind. The best part is that I ran into that locksmith, who was a legend in his own mine, at a local lock distributor. Again, he was bragging to a group that the Port was his and that the padlock bid would be in his pocket any day. He had it all sewed up and was just waiting for the paperwork to arrive.

I did not have the heart to show him the Port contract in my pocket; I just nodded and smiled; he would find out soon enough.

As I delivered the hardware and software and my expertise to the port, I was careful to point out to the director that the terminals could be converted to this key system, assuring smooth access across the port for officers and maintenance personnel in an emergency. Tenants would be keyed into the system with an elevated level of security. What a wonderful idea they all agreed, and the port became mine, all mine.

# Chapter 26
# Coyotes

COYOTES

Driving is a thing in my occupation, and I can cover long distances between jobs. I found myself one year spending hours driving between Charleston and Myrtle Beach up the coast. The trip would take me over a couple of bridges in the small city of Georgetown on the eastern coast. Low hung bridges that span a couple of rivers in the PeeDee Basin.

Passing over the bridges one day I glanced down and noticed a couple of tugs juggling into position a new aluminum floating dock of substantial size. Anchoring it to pilings I noticed there was no gangway to access the platforms and that the bank was marsh and mud with no buildings.

I would drive back and forth for about a week, until one day returning home I glanced down at the floating dock and noticed a large yellow dog standing on the new aluminum structure with ears blowing in the breeze. Happy dog I thought, then after reviewing the event in my head I concluded not a dog but a wild coyote that had somehow accessed the boat dock.

Having the good fortune to be working a large project in Myrtle Beach, I found myself the next day passing the same spot on the way home. Curious I looked and now I saw there were two coyotes on the platforms. I assumed it must have trudged through the muck and swam the short distance to climb up on the boat dock. Possible they were mates and couldn't bear to be separated.

A few days passed before I had the opportunity to pass that way again. And yes, there they were still stranded on the dock. This was unbelievable to me. Perhaps they couldn't get back to shore and were sleeping and living a trapped life of hopelessness. Surely hunger would soon drive them to return to the wild. Maybe a kind boater would offer them passage, not sure if I would allow wild coyotes on my boat I thought.

A few more days passed before I passed over that bridge and I strained my neck to see if the dogs or more possible, the coyotes had managed a escape.


NO! They had not. One lay dead sprayed out on its side, large red tongue hanging out of its mouth on the hot metal deck. Eyes not blinking, flys swarming and the second animal standing at a distance possible in shock and knowing its time was coming also for the cruel hands of death.

And now I was passed the bridge, my eyes filling with tears, I hated myself. I could of, I should of done more, something. I love dogs and coyotes were just wild dogs that deserved more then just a hot horrible death at the hands of hunger.

Wait! I realized that there was still one animal alive on that dock. You must do something. Pulling off to the side of the road and wiping the tears from my eyes, I grabbed my cellphone and searched for some Animal rescue or SPCA. Anyone who loved Animals as much as I.

Finally, I reached some local branch of the SPCA, and a kind woman answered the phone. At first I must have been babbling, but soon I conveyed the facts of a poor lonely coyote that had lost her mate and needed rescue before the sun could go down. She would not survive one more day and this was all my fault. I'm lazy, selfish, and stupid please, please save this animal.

The woman just laughed at me. Laughed. "Oh Sir! Sir! she just kept saying. We've had hundreds of calls on those two Coyotes." I was affronted by her callous attitude. "Well, why haven't you done something to save those poor dogs?" I was yelling. "you're the SPCA."

And the poor women just laughing, said, "Sir, those coyotes are fake! Stuffed! Not real". "They are on the dock to scare away the birds."

And suddenly all my anger and guilt and disgust with myself was gone. The coyotes were going to be okay.

Chapter 27

# Dimes to Diamonds

Dimes to Diamonds

Wealth, money, the stuff we like to wallow in, wade through, throw it up in the air, the good stuff. It is measured in various commodities, cash, gold, stocks, bonds, and even diamonds. What makes someone wealthy is as diverse as human nature. How much, is up to personal interpretation. Whatever 'it' is, I have learned that others desire 'it' and want to take that away from you, the one who has 'it.' Wealth breeds dishonesty, thievery, mistrust, deception, violence, and murder, and that is naming only a few of the character flaws that come to my mind.

The first question that comes up, if you possess anything of value is, how do I hang on to it, keep it safe, maintain my wealth? The attacks on your valuables may come at any time, from anyone, any direction. We all have seen family members turn on one another when the time to divide the wealth of a passing relative is at hand, actions that are despicable to watch, the hatred between siblings' heart-breaking. The constant bombardment of cyber attacks to pry information from us, to access our bank accounts or defraud us of our home title. The child who steals your car in the middle of the night, only to wake up and find it 'totaled' in your driveway, the child sound asleep in bed.

Security is the tool for us to provide protection for our wealth and ourselves and that is the profession in which I am involved. As a locksmith I am involved in the physical protection of your assets. To protect and control the access points to your wealth, the doors, the windows, the safes. I am aware that security is a layered approach for true security. I help to control entry, but electronic security is as important. Alarms that monitor late hours and provide fire detection fit in with CCTV that stands surveillance twenty-four hours, three hundred and sixty-five days each year. Access control devices tied in with physical hardware will control key entry points and tied to computers and cloud-based software the combinations and possibilities are endless.

Larger projects will hire a security consultant to design and layer all available options to thwart perceived attacks that could happen. From firewalls to fire suppression collaborating with consultants in the design of these systems is challenging and fun. It should involve all phases of the buildout, including alarm experts, construction managers, electricians and me, your local hardware supplier and installer.

One big monkey wrench in designing security is life safety codes. Life safety takes precedents over security, and no matter how much the desire to secure an exit point, free egress almost always rules. The NAPA101 fire and life safety codes teamed up with an overzealous Fire Marshall have ruined many a young man's day. The best part is that interpretation of the code is at the discretion of the local fire inspector. Some of these fire inspectors have never read the code or misinterpret what they read. Your project is at the whim of a local code inspector and there is no avenue for review.

I worked on a large project one time for a Savy diamond merchant out of New York. He had built a large warehouse from scratch that housed, at its core, a vault the size of a basketball court.

My job for him was the building of Man traps. Two for pedestrian traffic and a third for the UPS truck that made daily deliveries. A man trap is usually a series of three doors and when you pass through the first door, controlled by a security agent, doors two and three lock down. Once in the first cubicle you are trapped until the guard allows door two to open. Doors one and three lock down until door two closes. You move forward to a second cubicle and wait for the guard to admit entrance through door three. Cameras watch over the procession and with this job we installed thick bullet proof glass to view the portals from the adjacent control station. With red and green lights to control the flow of foot traffic, you would pass through armored doors that weighed upwards of five hundred pounds. The UPS mantrap worked with motorized roll up gates built with control panels, lights for access and limit switches.

Always working and doing upgrades to the numerous systems for the diamond merchant, I noticed an unordinary number of packages going out constantly through the day, and I asked the Security office once, "why so many?" He responded that most of the packages were empty, only one contained merchandise. If someone were going to "jack" a shipment they would need a crystal ball to get the right one.

He had a delivery vehicle, old, rusted, and dirty. Dents and faded paint, a cracked windshield, I asked the owner with all his money why he did not buy a new car for his company. "Ray" he said, "Lift the hood." I did and under the hood a spotless V-8 motor appeared. New wide tires with deep tread and shocks that were heavy duty, strong.

He claimed it had enough horsepower to outrun a corvette. Then it dawned on me, this car was a diversion, camouflage, a leopard with spots. Who would ever expect this relic of an automobile to be carrying diamonds or gold? Yet if ever pressed by robbers it had enough "Gizmo and Guts" to escape a deadly scenario.

In his security design of the building, the concrete walls had steel plates to prevent breeching by force. I noticed that the interior of the walls had vibration sensors and noise monitors. The ceiling was protected as well and only fake windows on the exterior. Of course, he had cameras everywhere with state-of-the-art software to control them. Even the Plenum air space from the roof to the drop-down ceiling tiles had cameras should someone choose this space to hide.

What I loved most was that all employees worked inside the vault building jewelry for television. To go inside the vault, you would need to walk into this large boxlike structure to be weighted. Weighted to a tenth of an ounce. You would be weighted also when leaving, and the goal was that the weights had to match, or you weighted less due to perspiration.

This operation was the ultimate in security, and I have seen some good ones.

Working in bank security, I learned that layered security is always at the forefront in loss prevention. Lowlifes always paint a target on financial institutes, but robbing a bank is a federal crime and seldom is the "take" worth the risk. Federal crimes involves the FBI, and capture is only a matter of time. I would not want those guys looking for me. Remember the television show with the theme song, "if you can't do the time, don't do the crime."

To be honest there is not much money in banks. Banks keep their money in centrally located money houses. These warehouses of money are non-descript and invisible to the general public. The only clue to their existence is the occasional armored car that enters an electronically controlled bay door. If you were to look closer, you could see surveillance cameras mounted on the outside of the warehouse but no signage indicating what activities were being conducted on its interior. No loose bills blowing in the wind.

In Miami I visited numerous money houses to improve or repair some of the physical locking devices or repair a camera. Mantraps are used extensively at these locations and also at armored car locations. Vaults with multiple dials and time locks are common and in constant need of service. Large men packing big guns and sour dispositions greet you at the entrance. You must present credentials, a metal detection device wanded over your body, and your tool bag emptied and examined. You walk through various mantrap doors and work with an escort. When done and leaving the process is reversed.

Working at a money warehouse location in Miami, I witnessed a warehouse that was divided into multiple rooms roughly twelve feet by twelve feet, each room with multiple cameras hanging from the ceiling. Guessing on the count, I estimated four dozen rooms. The rooms had homemade benches that were wrapped around the interior, and all had glass windows extending from a three-foot height to the ceiling. On those benches were stacked bundles of money. Bills of different denominations from the countertop to the height of the ceiling. Most bundles of money were wrapped in plastic wrap, mountains of cash, from the wall to the edge of the bench, from the bench to the white drop ceiling. I never saw so much green, so much money.

I was called to the director's office to discuss the scope of my work and upon entering the manager's office, he extended a chair, and I sat down across from him at his desk to discuss what he needed done. It was hard to ignore that his desk had money strewn everywhere. Fifties and hundreds were the predominate denomination, an occasional twenty would pop out. Stacks and wads of large bills were strewed across his desk and over the dark green carpet covering the floor. As we talked an armored vehicle pulled up to the rolldown door. Observing the truck on the large CCTV monitor, the driver honked his horn. The Manager excused himself to greet the driver and receive a new shipment. Leaving me alone he promised to return shortly.

I will admit I was nervous sitting there with all that money, large bills, casually waffling in the air. Accumulating in the corners of the room like large green dust balls. I started feeling feint and weak in my knees. Life was being very cruel to me at that moment.

Finally, the man returned and sat back down behind his desk. With anger in my voice, "Damn you!" I told him. "Do not ever leave me alone like this. You got money floating in the air and your desk is piled high with bills in no conceivable order. That is too much temptation!" I cried.

He started laughing and laughing, and with tears streaming down his face he explained, "All the money in this room, is counterfeit! Useless."

Worked in a money room one day in Fort Lauderdale fixing locks for a major national bank. I walked into a large back room and two men were inside. One was down in a large deep pit with a snow shovel scooping up quarters and tossing them into a wheelbarrow. The other man would take the heavily loaded wheelbarrow and roll it up a ramp over to a smaller second pit, and dump it in, and a mechanical machine under the second pit would whirl and spin to sort and roll the coins. Spitting out neatly rolled coins in some mysterious location. If I had not seen it, I would not have believed it.

One day my parents invited me over to their new house for dinner. They were extra nice to me, which was quite unusual, and I realized something was up. After one of my mom's infamous meals and Dad's inane banter they both suddenly looked me in the eye and assumed a solemn tone. Mom explained that they had moved in and found a floor safe under the carpet in their bedroom closet. Mom and Dad had not been able to sleep nights not knowing what mystery lay inside that sealed container, in their closet. Was that the motive for inviting me for dinner?

Yes, you guessed correctly. Could I get it open, was their pressing question. "We believe it's full of cash," my mother gushed. "No," my dad said "it has gold rings and emerald bracelets. Possibly a sapphire broach." "Please," they pleaded, "go get your tools and hurry right back."

'Well, Mom and Dad" I started, "I hate to disillusion you guys, but I do twenty or thirty of these a year, and almost always they are empty. I'll go and get my tools, but do not get so excited. It's bound to be empty."

I walked to my service truck and retrieved my drill and tools. On a full stomach I painfully crouched down and started working my magic. Within thirty minutes the safe was ready to open. I gripped the small handle and pulled open the lid to the small floor safe. Mom and dad fell over me trying to peer inside the dark cavity in the floor.

It was empty! Such disappointment, all their dreams evaporating on the humid evening air. Both looked at me as if it were my fault the safe was empty. I reached down inside the dark can and ran my hand across the bottom, "Wait!' I cried, "I found something." And pulling my hand from the safe, between my fingers I held a thin silver dime.

"You are disgusting!" they said to me. And that is my dime story. It was a long time before they invited me back over for dinner.

STORYAPERTURE.COM

FOLLOW  US  ON

www.ingramcontent.com/pod-product-compliance
Lightning Source LLC
Chambersburg PA
CBHW071424300726
48976CB00004B/1231